Mimi Bryant

S0-AGQ-838

KAMONGO

OR

THE LUNGFISH AND THE PADRE

Also by Homer W. Smith

THE END OF ILLUSION

MAN AND HIS GODS

FROM FISH TO PHILOSOPHER

KAMONGO

OR, THE LUNGFISH AND THE PADRE

by Homer W. Smith

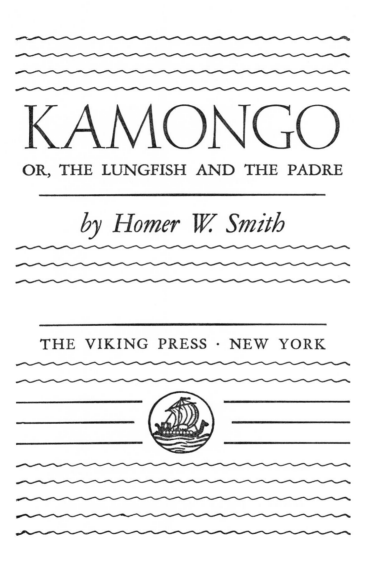

THE VIKING PRESS · NEW YORK

COPYRIGHT 1932, 1949, COPYRIGHT © RENEWED 1965
BY HOMER W. SMITH

ALL RIGHTS RESERVED

VIKING COMPASS EDITION AUGUST 1956

DISTRIBUTED IN CANADA BY
THE MACMILLAN COMPANY OF CANADA LIMITED

ELEVENTH PRINTING NOVEMBER 1973

SBN 670-00011-6

LIBRARY OF CONGRESS CATALOG CARD NUMBER: 49-16261

PRINTED IN THE U.S.A. BY THE COLONIAL PRESS INC.

to

C. G. S.

KAMONGO

OR

THE LUNGFISH AND THE PADRE

I

HE shout of a sailor awakened him and Joel opened his eyes to peer into the blackness beyond the aura of the deck-lights. He could barely distinguish the faint colour of the sandy shore and, above it, the dark shadows of trees outlined against the sky. He heard a winch wheezing as a boat was lowered forward, and men's voices as they unhooked the lines and rowed away from the ship.

He turned his head quickly to either side as though apprehensive someone might be watching him. He had only one companion—on his right an Anglican priest was stretched, like himself, in a long canvas deck-chair. Far aft, hidden in the shadows cast by the feeble yellow lamps, there were other recumbent figures relaxed in sleep. A hand here, a face there was struck by the light and stood out pallidly in the shadows. He got up slowly and walked over to the side of the deck. Once outside the light of the covered passage his eyes took in the narrow strip of black water which separated the ship from the shore, and beyond it, softly lit by the brilliant stars, the grey outlines of sand-dunes rolling back to where a few palms and feathery trees were silhouetted against the sky. After a moment of searching he made out the figures of several sailors who were hauling on a ship's line, preparatory to making her fast to the piles that were set at intervals along the bank of the canal. Quietly, so as not to disturb his companion, he stepped back into the shadows and crossed the deck; but he returned almost immediately and, straddling his deck-chair, dropped into it heavily as though he had returned from a fatiguing journey.

"Another tanker?"

Joel looked around at the priest.

"Sorry, did I wake you? Yes, we are tying up again. We'll be lucky if we get into Saïd before dawn."

The priest looked at his watch. "Nine-thirty. Yes, we'll have breakfast in Port Saïd. Do you know that we have been asleep for two hours?" He laughed as he added: "I feel as though it had been ten."

Joel smiled but remained silent as he let his glance rest upon his companion, who was wiping his moist face with a handkerchief. The priest was a big man, broad-shouldered and straight, at least three inches taller than Joel and probably a few years older. Joel guessed him to be about thirty-three. He was smooth-shaven and his regular features and tanned skin suggested a soldier who had spent most of his life in the open. He was dressed in black broadcloth coat and trousers and a black waistcoat buttoned up closely around a stiff white collar. But in spite of his heavy clothes he seemed to feel nothing of the oppressive heat.

Joel took out a handkerchief and, mopping his own face and neck, looked down at himself, at the soft slippers on his feet, the linen trousers clinging limply to his legs, and the wrinkled coat soiled from restless contortions in a deck-chair. His hand went self-consciously to his neck, caressing the throat within the open collar. He wondered how long it had been since he had worn a tie. So he had slept two hours? Well, it was the first two hours in a long, long time. But he did feel better, at that. He pushed himself out in an all-embracing stretch and slowly enjoyed the delight of the muscular movement.

He rose stiffly, still stretching, toning the muscles of his arms and shoulders, and walked over to the edge of the deck. Resting his arms upon the rail he leaned out to peer through the darkness at the sand-dunes. A cur got up out of the band of light and slunk into the shadows to lie down beside some white-robed figures chattering in Arabic. A faint breath of air touched his cheek. He closed his eyes and turned his face upward as though he could confirm the impression by his sense of smell. In the darkness of his concentration the breeze came again, neither cool nor warm, without sensory quality, but like a ghostly hand brushing lightly across his face. So that was why he had slept? Cool! Cool!

The relief of moving air! The unrest, the muscular tension that had pervaded him slipped away gradually before a sense of well-being, of sheer animal comfort. His head dropped forward and his shoulders rose and fell in deep, deliberate respirations. His mind, awakening as the physical strain passed off, ran back as though unreeling a belated record that moved quickly past his indifferent attention.

Nearly a week ago they had come to anchor at Aden. . . . Weary of the ship's monotony, they went ashore hoping to find some diversion and to get a decent drink. A decent drink, uhh! All they got was a warm, sweet lemon squash because the hotels had run out of ice! There was nothing for them to do but wander from one curio store to another; to stare at the water-carts that were dragged along the hot asphalt streets by slobbering camels; to push off the eternal obsequious venders of junk that slithered out of every shadow to importune the stranger; to shut their eyes against the glare from white walls and white, sterile dust, and to wonder why in the world the British wanted Aden. . . .

Bored with the dust and heat and flies, somebody

suggested that they motor through the mountain pass and up to the Wells of Solomon. So they went along the tourist trail, a motley string of trippers dressed in white duck, black broadcloth, tweeds, linen, sun-hats, terais, climbing over the flanks of the crumbling hills that rise abruptly out of the Desert of Arabia. Old weathered peaks, worn into sharp hog-backs and deep crevasses by the wind and rain, with jagged shoulders decorated in many colours by Nature's hieroglyphics. Across the deep ravines the Wells of Solomon looked like giant buttresses set in to keep the hills apart; curving walls and deep pits built by some forgotten Persian—and recently veneered with modern rock and mortar by the optimistic British— to keep back the rain, they rise up tier after tier across the sheer gorges like a gargantuan honeycomb thrown down for ants to scramble over. Gigantic vats—could they be filled with water the desert down below might blossom in green squares of palms and patches of exotic flowers. But not in the memory of man had they been filled, not in five years had their dust been wet by rain. . . . Tremendous industry made futile by a shift in wind!

They went back to the ship, satiated with the desert landscape, to loll upon the deck and fan themselves despairingly while they stared up at the mountains around them; barren mountains pitted with decay and ribbed with broad fans of rotten rock, fired into red and yellow colours by the setting sun. Sea, rock, and sky confused to make a quivering mist, unreal, unearthly. It might have been the gate to Hell, itself!

Being French, the *Dumbea* had crossed the Arabian Sea to call Djibuti, as though it were not enough to pass through this torrid penance without prolonging it. From sundown to sunup she steamed across a barely broken sea, her passengers tossing in their bunks in a vain effort to sleep, or pacing the decks waiting for the dawn.

But when that dawn came it was like the splitting of the heavens. Naked, white, the light came down as though even the blanket of thin air above them had been torn away; the world seemed to be taken up and engulfed in the sun's incandescent substance. As the *Dumbea* made her way through the elongated channel of Djibuti Harbour the tar flowed in her deck-seams and her woodwork burned the flesh. She might have been a furnace belching heat rather than a ship taking it in. Her human cargo came sprawling out of her and wandered restlessly from shadow to shadow, mopping—fanning—mopping—fanning.

Boredom and curiosity can drive men to absurd ends, Joel thought, but it was neither of these that had driven them ashore that midday. To suffer in confinement is a double agony; to move about and curse and move again brings some relief. They had not expected to be cooled by walking into the doors of that furnace; they had not expected the parched hills and choking dust of Somaliland to bring forth a cooling spring to meet their need as had the rock of Horeb beneath the Hebrew's staff. No, they had simply rushed from the hot ship into the hotter town as they might have danced about upon a searing griddle.

Joel laughed as he recalled the picture of himself struggling along the dusty road to fetch a taxi to the landing wharf, pushing through the blinding glare as though it were something fluid, corporeal. Exhausted at the end, he threw himself down in the shadow of a wall to rest—but only to rise hastily from sand too hot to bear against his body.

They found some relief in the darkness of the hotel bar—coatless, collars open, sleeves rolled back, mopping, fanning, beating off the flies. They drank innumerable Tom Collinses, with ice, real ice, long bitter drinks of lime and gin that wet the mouth and cooled the gullet and that sent faint waves of coldness down the back and arms. Under the eaves and through the shutters the white light poured, radiated by a world whitewashed with liquid fire. They drank and joked and mopped and drank again, and begged the boy to work the punkah faster, faster! They thrust their hands from under cover to appraise the naked sun—and hurried back to drink again. From the shadows of tiled roofs that broke its force they cursed the heat, their bodies stretched out before the slowly swinging fan, drinking its air, seeking its caress, living by it. To sweat was to endure, to defeat the demoniacal energy of that broiling oven. . . . But what, when sweat should be of no avail? They sensed, as they climbed back aboard the ship, avoiding its hot iron and hunting out its shadows, that they were further cursed, that punkahs could no longer save them.

The dinner-gong rang as the *Dumbea* rounded the outflung arm of Somaliland hills and turned her course into the Red Sea. The land fall was a prismatic band around the horizon, violet near the water and blending in yellow and gold above, where the light struck off at an angle from the peaks. Bearing a thin, levelled streak of cloud across its face the sun glared through the red haze of dust as though charged with living hatred. Defeated in its efforts to annihilate it seemed to promise a renewed attack, sharpened by accumulated cunning, on the morrow. The walls of the ship threw their radiation against the body as though there were so little room for that all-pervading fluid in them that it must be poured with increased concentration into the haggard bodies of men and the dark spaces where they tried to hide. At the thresholds of the companionways there hung a curtain of intolerable warmth, a blast that by its greater force arrested them. It stank of vile things, long dead, hardly remembered things buried in the ship's bowels and now stirred up like ghosts to seek the outside air. Men wandered disconsolately toward the shadowed doors to stop arrested by the pall; until driven by the urgency of despair, monotony, or human need they bent their heads and forced themselves into the nether world.

Like a thin veneer, Joel thought, our pleasure is spread upon the base of vital needs, thinning or thickening as the animal beneath thrusts up or draws below the level of attention. But even the lowest state of living demands distraction, demands that the sheer monotony of consciousness be shattered here and there by some diversion. Men forced themselves into the stifling ship to eat and drink, no longer from an honest need but because the mind, in order to endure, requires that it be fed a pabulum of sense and be permitted to exercise itself in motion, however futile. So they ate and drank even while their clothes clung to their bodies with wet transparency, and the sweat matted their hair and ran down their faces in little rivulets to drop off into their food. They became nauseated with the smell and rushed back on deck, swearing that they would not go below again.

They wandered aimlessly up and down the ship or threw themselves into their chairs with complete exhaustion. They took off their coats, their collars and their shoes and left their legs outstretched to block the road of passers-by. They mopped their faces and arms and shoulders and hung their handkerchiefs upon the rail or waved them slowly back and forth to get them dry; and when they would not dry they mopped with them wet, and cursed the eternal sweat that ran down their bodies in perpetual streams. They looked up as though expecting to see the oppressive blanket that enveloped them but there was only the blue sky; never a cloud, never a bird but only the funnel smoke rising straight and then curving back to disappear into the haze; and on every side only the darker blue oily water, rolling a little. They thought of the soldiers cooped up in the steerage, six to a cabin with hardly enough deck-space to stand in, and only heavy woollen clothes to wear. They wondered how they survived the stifling heat. But they were not moved to pity, only casual curiosity. It was too hot to pity anybody, even the woman pacing the deck with her baby, incessantly muttering, *"Mon enfant, mon enfant, regarde l'eau!"*

By night they dragged their mattresses on deck and stared up at the stars which swayed from side to side in a perpetual, nauseating motion. They looked down at the sea and saw the stars, swaying again. They wondered where the air began and sea left off. Throughout the endless hours they tossed and turned, their bodies leaving pools of water behind them when they moved. Under the dim aura of the night-lamps the deck-boards were brown with wetness and the rails dripped, dripped an incandescent dew.

Day after day, sunup, sundown, the *Dumbea* pushed on through the slightly rolling water. . . . The old Russian Count was the first to go: they took up a collection to buy him a tin coffin so that he could be buried at home. The ship's carpenter hastily soldered him in it, the while cursing and dripping with perspiration over the hot torch and soldering iron. Then two of the stokers followed the Russian into hastily soldered coffins. Lascars they were, for even Negroes cannot stand the heat; Lascars who drink salt water to replace the salt they lost in sweat . . . then two soldiers . . . and the little cockney barber from Dar-es-Salaam had almost gone—he had been picked up in the bar and carried to his bunk, pallid and in collapse. For twelve hours the men had taken turns fanning his white body until he came around. . . . The children stood it best, but always in torment from the big red weals of heat-rash, crying,

crying throughout the night. . . . Night after night, pacing the deck or lying in a pool of sweat . . . if you could only sleep . . . Christ, sleep. . . .

Joel straightened up and rubbed his eyes and arms. He turned back to his companion. "So we slept two hours?"

The Padre was staring off into the darkness seeing, perhaps, some bit of England miraged above the sands of Egypt. "I did," he answered after a moment of blankness, laughing. "Didn't you?"

"Dead to the world!" Joel replied. "Two hours isn't much, but it helps." He came back to his chair and stretched out in it. The Padre had fallen back into his meditation, his eyes fixed on his toes which he was slowly moving back and forth. Joel tried to recall if he had once seen him during that appalling week without his coat, or even without that stiff white collar. The man seemed to be imperturbable, undaunted by the physical and mental strain that had played havoc with the rest of them. Was he insensible to physical discomfort, or did he possess some superhuman gift of fortitude?

"Does it get hot in Tanganyika? Like that?" he added, nodding his head back into time and space.

"No, not like that," the Padre answered. "That was the worst I've ever seen. It is indiscreet to come home by Suez in August. One should go around the Cape."

Joel laughed. "That's what the doctor said the Russian and the Lascars died of—indiscretion! Well—if I live through mine I intend to celebrate at Port Saïd. We'll have some coffee that hasn't been sea-sick for three months. How about it?"

He reached into his pocket and drew out a crumpled package of cigarettes and tried to light one. The cigarette refused to burn. He struck another match without success; so he took the cigarette out of his mouth and rolled it quizzically between his fingers.

The Padre was laughing at him: "It's got worm-holes in it. Didn't you know that there are special French worms that eat holes in French cigarettes?"

Joel bent the cigarette between his fingers as though it were elastic and in a sudden gesture of disgust and temper hurled it from him, but it fell short of the rail and rolled inconsequently into the scupper. The Padre laughed again at the violent but futile gesture.

"Let me get you a cigar," he said, and getting up out of his chair stiffly he disappeared into a nearby companionway. He returned shortly with an hermetically sealed humidor which he opened, giving Joel a cigar and taking one himself.

"Thanks, Padre. I'll reward you when we get to Saïd. Where'd you get them?"

"In Aden. They're not the best—but they haven't any

worm-holes, anyway. You know, I don't believe that worms like real tobacco."

"No, I don't think that you can hang the French tobacconists on that theory. Worms have queer tastes —I suppose as queer as the rest of us."

"Perhaps not, but my experience tells me that there is a presumption of guilt. I have kept cigars in Tanganyika for months and the only worms that ever got into them were big black ones, sneaking about on two legs. They put their white teeth into them and sneaked off into the bushes somewhere to smoke them. I've often hoped they were made beastly sick. You don't get many cigars in Tanganyika."

"No. Nor many other luxuries, I suppose?"

"No."

"Nor many necessities?"

"No . . . I had some books with me when I first went out, but I lost the lot of them on the way up. One of the canoes upset and spilled the boxes into the Ruvuma River. I had some more sent out from home, but it wasn't pleasant losing my few hand-picked books. Oh, I forgot—I had an almanac left, for which I was thankful."

"How long were the new ones coming?"

"About four months. It takes three weeks to get from Mwambo to Lukoniba. One has to walk most of the way because the river's not navigable. Then it's three or four days overland to the station. That is, in the dry season; it takes longer during the rains because you can't march in the afternoon. Then, too, you have to wait for a tramp steamer from Lindi down to Mwambo. We are in an out-of-the-way sort of place." He looked at Joel and half-way smiled with the last statement, as though he took some pride, like a frontiersman, in the inaccessibility of his post.

"And you have cigars there?"

"Most of the time. We get them sent up from Zanzibar. We have a lot of things—we have a gramophone now, and about thirty-five records; and two years ago when that expedition from Chicago came through shooting big game they left us a whopping big load of stuff—a field desk, three cots, some aluminum cooking utensils—of course, *they* weren't much good to us because our boys melted them on the fire the first thing-- but best of all, they left us an ice machine. Did you ever see one?"

Joel shook his head.

"You put some water—about a pint or a little more—into a container which fits in a copper ball, and then you turn a handle to freeze it. It takes about fifteen minutes to freeze it. I knew some physics once but I can't explain how the thing works—you know better than I do. I remember the first time we made ice with it—the stuff almost scared the life out of my *Mlahis*. They took one touch and then ran for their lives. Imagine never having touched anything cold! It still is a source of wonder to them. They pick up a piece of ice with a sheepish grin and then tear around in circles yelling their lungs out. I don't use it often, but it comes in very handy if one is sick.

"A lady friend of the Bishop's sent us up a set of tea things a year ago last Christmas. There were some tall glasses among them. I didn't know what they were for, but the Americans from Chicago said that they were for iced-tea—so we made iced-tea in honour of their visit. When the Bishop visited me a short time afterward I gave him some. He wouldn't believe it was meant to drink. Said it might give him cramps." The Padre laughed. "I don't believe it did, but he didn't come back to see me for nearly a year."

The missionary turned his attention to his cigar, which had gone out. Long after he stopped talking, it suddenly occurred to Joel that the Bishop was probably the only caller on his list. When he saw that the Padre had lapsed into silence, Joel rose and went over to the rail. He leaned across, looking ahead to where a low mound of black water was turned up by the ship's bow.

"We're under weigh again," he said over his shoulder.

A beam of light cut obliquely into the rounded top of the wave, making it a living, changing thing, yet fixed in form and space. Suddenly the water broke into a white foaming crest and as quickly melted back into its state of fixity. Somewhere a camel sneezed, but in the darkness there was no sign of life. Barely defined against the sky the land slipped by, hardly faster than a man might walk, the horizon rising and falling as barren hills gave way to barren valleys. Desert—where once had been green trees and giant beasts—now shifting, sterile sands where only man might venture in his providence. Desert—the very word meant deserted by life, where life could not live. There were places where life could live—and there was desert. Life could live in the hills, in jungles, in swamps, in plains, in meadows, in lakes and rivers, and in the sea—but there were places in the hills and in the valleys and even in the lakes and in the sea where life could not live—great vacuums of death like the interstellar spaces. They were laid with the curse of death for lack of water, soil, air, or heat. Water, earth, air, and fire—four elements. Joel shuddered; what a horror when they met in disproportion!

II

J OEL lay back in his deck-chair, his eyes set into the night, his fingers idly stroking the deck beneath him while he puffed on the cigar in the corner of his mouth. He suddenly took the cigar out and examined its ash interestedly.

"The ancients' idea that the world was flat and that if we went too far we'd fall off was not a bad one. Symbolic, in a way. Expressed our limitations. They sensed—" he shrugged his shoulders "—no less than we do, I suppose, the narrow margin in this scheme of things in which we live. We've just been crowded to the narrow edge— crowded between Africa and Arabia until we almost fell off."

The Padre turned his head sideways and studied Joel's face, as though this might help him to understand what he was talking about.

"You mean crowded physically?" he asked.

"Well—crowded physiologically," Joel explained. "You can be crowded in a lot of ways, but they all have

20

the same result in the long run. If you get crowded **too** much you fall off."

The Padre nodded his head and turned back to examine the ashes of his cigar.

"Yes." He leaned forward to flip the ash into the scupper. "You're always crowded in there." He indicated by a slight movement of his head that he referred to the vast continent of Africa, rather than the meagre sea, behind them. "Crowded one way or another. The margin is a narrow one. I wonder why men go into Africa—when there are so many happy places, glad, joyous, singing—" He glanced at Joel with a look that seemed to say: "Isn't it strange?" or, "Am I not right . . . ?"

Joel shook his head by way of answering generally this general question; then it occurred to him that the way the Padre had put it required something more than this negligent dismissal.

"Well—" he raised his eyebrows and made a gesture that clearly turned the question back upon his companion.

"Oh, I had good reasons." The Padre laughed self-consciously. "But one can't very well put them into words. They are difficult to define and—they run far back into the roots of my life. They are—" he sought a moment for the word, "fundamental. Oh! you know what I mean—the kind of thing that you grow up with, like your language; that is built into you from the very beginning."

Joel was puzzled by this declaration. It somehow did not fit the youthful, active character of the man. Surely he didn't take himself so seriously as to believe that it was a sort of unavoidable destiny—this missionary work. He was not that sort. Why the devil had he gone in for it, anyway? It didn't fit him; he should have been an engineer, or a surgeon, or an archæologist.

Damn it all, Joel thought, you never got below the surface with him. He seemed to be wrapped around by some impregnable armour of silence, like the vacuum around a thermos jar. Once, on a Sunday just out of Mombasa, he had held a morning service on the ship and had come to Joel with a polite: "Would like to have you come." He had the delicacy, the tact, to put it that way, and not to say, "Will you come?" It would have been embarrassing if he had not. From the beginning of the voyage he and Joel had spent most of the time to-gether; they gravitated to each other, for some strange reason, as deck-companions and they found each other's company so agreeable that they just sat together and watched the days go by, talking leisurely and discon-nectedly about Africa, England, Prohibition, anything. It would have been embarrassing had he said, "Will you come?" But when he put it indirectly Joel had just said, "Thanks, Padre," and the event had not been mentioned again. Joel's default had not made the slightest difference in their relations. It was swallowed up in that vacuum-like, silent acquiescence that insulated the man. That was one reason why Joel liked him. He was good-humoured, but tactful about it!

Joel wondered why he thought of him as silent, for he was not literally silent—he was, in fact, an easy and intelligent talker. Might it be that there was some deep contentment that pervaded his superficial moods? And yet, contentment was not quite the word, for there was something about him, something in his voice, that suggested discontent, unhappiness, as though he were, or had been, crowded by an oppressive world. But certainly one could not think of him as being crowded in any vulgar sense; he was too well turned-out, too Oxonian, too suave, soigné. No, any crowding here was inside, spirit subtly crowding spirit. The man puzzled him. His whole character belied the superficial inference from his cloth: he was no evangelical fanatic but a man of scholarship, culture, power; a man who viewed the world with an unprejudiced eye and judged it in a reasonable sort of way. He was a man to like, to tie to.

He was a man who should appreciate the treacherous depths of mysticism, the shallowness of ritual; who should not hold the ignorantly muttered prayers of savages as worth a candle. It was difficult to think of him as teaching savages to pray, or buying their supplications with mingled threats of Hell and promises of Heaven, spreading around himself a shallow sham of power, superiority, beneficence. He was no Glory-to-God man! You simply could not imagine him supplicating, cringing, begging. Rather, you expected to find him suppliant before the mystery of the jungle, searching among the native ways, the old wives' tales and secret stores of myth for a light of understanding to shine upon the savages he had gone out to teach; you expected to find him engaged with the analysis, dissection, reassembling of the obscure life of some barbaric bushman, holding it in his clear vision alongside that of old Greece or Gaul.

But no—he might be these, but, first of all—he was devout. . . . And therein lay the paradox. . . .

Joel wondered again why he had gone in for this sort of thing. There was something in his voice that suggested regret and disillusion. . . . "So many happy places, glad, joyous, singing" . . . The forests of Africa were not happy places. Life was hard, lonely, barren. A man had to find everything within himself when it was two hundred miles to the nearest white man, two hundred miles to share a wish, a word, a memory; two months from friendly face to friendly face. It took a powerful force to send a man—an intelligent man—into that sort of life. And this man was, certainly, intelligent. It might have been a great adventure when he first went out, but he was going back! Going back again to a round clearing in a Tanganyika forest to be alone in a rude hut with a meagre pile of books, a rough temple dedicated to his God, and with his memories—memories of the world, of friends, of things, joyous, happy things; to be alone with his desires, his aches, his pains, to be alone with his unutterable loneliness. Was it to take to his uncomprehending savages some part of himself, some twig of the spiritual vegetation that grew up in him, rooted in the humus of the past; some mystic twig of an all-healing herb that was supposed to bless the recipient with Eternal Life, Salvation? Joel remembered a parade he had once seen in Mombasa: a string of shiftless, barefoot blacks dressed in rags and tatters of European clothes had come tramping down the dusty street one afternoon with a clamour of drums and bugles. Toward the end of the column a dirty white banner proclaimed: "JESUS SAVES."

It was inconceivable that this man could take that kind of thing seriously! Joel gave him up as beyond his comprehension.

He suddenly realized that the Padre was staring at him, that they were staring at each other without acknowledgment, each wondering what sort of man the other was.

"And you?" the Padre asked without taking his eyes away.

"Oh, my reasons were very simple," said Joel, laughing. "I went to Africa to—well, to fish. Not for sport, but on a sort of scientific fishing trip. To get lungfish."

The Padre seemed to be waiting for some enlargement on this statement, so Joel added: "I've been there before—two years ago. My wife and I went to Kisumu, on Lake Victoria, after some of these same fish and took a number of them home with us. I've just been back to get more so that I could keep on with my work."

"Oh, I see. For a museum. You are an ichthyologist——"

"No, a physiologist."

The Padre acknowledged the technical correction with a slight nod of his head. "I've heard strange reasons for men going to Africa, but I think that is the strangest—to come all this way for one fish. Couldn't you have had them sent to you?"

"No, I had to come and get them. I took them home alive, you see. I had to have them alive for my purposes. They are peculiar fish. They are called lungfish because they breathe by means of both lungs and gills. They live in the rivers and lakes but when the dry season comes, if they are trapped in the swamps, they dig into the mud and lie buried until the rains come along and cover the land with water again. They can live in the hard mud, breathing by means of their lungs, for months, years—almost in a state of suspended animation. Starving, waiting, hanging on—crowded," Joel laughed, "as we were yesterday, by an inexorable Nature."

"They are queer creatures. It's strange I never heard of them. Where do they live?"

"In Lake Victoria, Lake Albert, the White Nile—you should have them down your way in Tanganyika. They are found in almost all the rivers and lakes of Equatorial Africa. There is another species that lives in the Belgian Congo and a third that lives up in Gambia. Rather local, spotted distribution. There's a closely related genus in Australia and another in South America. They live—they always have lived, I think—only in fresh water, never in the sea. The Australian species is quite scarce, nearly extinct, in fact. The natives like to eat them and the Government has had to put them under protection. . . . Government staving off the evil day when they will be crowded out, for good!

"They once"—Joel turned in his chair, his interest in his subject drawing him closer to his listener—"were wide-spread over the world. That was in a geologically remote time when the continents were fused or connected together. Their fossils have been found in Europe, Asia, Malaya, Australia, North and South America, Africa. Four hundred million years ago they were the cream of life, lords of creation; pioneers in a new way of living, escaping the threat of death that lurks in droughts, stagnant pools, poisoned waters, through breathing air by means of their newly invented lungs. But they have remained almost unchanged through the ages, carrying on in the old way of living until now they are largely crowded out, just a few stragglers hanging on to the very edge of annihilation. Life has gone around them, leaving them behind. They are like living pages out of life's history."

When Joel stopped a feeling of embarrassment came over him. He was irritated by his own loquaciousness. Why should he burst out in a long harangue to a stranger casually inquiring about a thing of interest? Scientific evangelism! That's what it amounted to, and that kind was as bad as any other. He looked over at his companion, wondering what sort of a pushing ass he might think him to be. But the Padre was leaning forward, his chin cupped in his hands, looking out into the night. He had never seen the man until two weeks ago. But the past week—there had been something to throw them together. He had completely forgotten the oppression that he had thought would hang on to him for days. It seemed now unreal, an evil dream dissolving in a wakening moment. He walked over to the rail and looked ahead, searching for the lights of Ismaïlia that would come up out of the night somewhere to the northwest. The breeze had become stronger, more definite and perceptibly cool. The sandy hills that were moving past seemed to have been piled up by a steam-shovel at regular intervals.

"What do they look like?"

The Padre's voice took him by surprise and a moment intervened before he could reassemble the man and his question. Joel turned around:

"Oh, the fish! . . . They are rather eel-shaped, round and elongated with rope-like fins. They are olive-brown or black above and greyish underneath. Their heads are blunt, like a snake's, with massive jaws and flat teeth designed for crushing snail-shells. The natives say that they can bite a broom-handle in two, but that's an exaggeration. However, I'd hate to get my fingers snapped by a big one. There is a mounted specimen in the Nairobi Museum seven feet long. He looks the part of a prehistoric monster! The natives believe that they are a 'cross' between a fish and a crocodile—not a strange association when you see one flopping around on the ground, opening his frightful jaws to take a breath."

"They must be a 'cross' between a fish and some land

animal, judging from the way they live; and you say they breathe by means of lungs. Other fishes don't have lungs, do they?"

"The higher fishes did have lungs once; or rather they are descended from ancient forms which did. It was also from those ancient air-breathing fishes that the first land animals evolved. This lungfish, though modified in some ways, is the closest surviving remnant of the ancestral stock that gave rise to the modern fishes on the one hand and the terrestrial animals on the other. The fishes have, for the most part, discarded the archaic lung or made it over into an air-tight gas bag or swim-bladder. While the terrestrial animals have kept the lung, and improved upon it."

"Why is he—your lungfish—so important to you?"

"For two reasons: first, because of the peculiar life he leads. When the dry season comes and the swamplands dry out, he buries himself beneath the mud and engages in a long-time fast. Many animals hibernate in the winter-time when it is cold but the lungfish goes to sleep in his mud nest, or æstivates, during the hottest months of the year. He is imprisoned there until the rains come again and set him free. The mud around him dries as hard as rock so that he could not, if he wanted it, get anything to eat. So, of course, he has to burn his own tissues for fuel like any other fasting animal, to keep alive. I believe he takes the prize as fasting champion, because he can certainly last for several years, perhaps for five, if he is fat enough when he goes into æstivation. Then, too, he has no water in his earthbound prison and consequently his kidneys have to stop working. All the products of his metabolism pile up in his blood and tissues—a condition that would kill all other animals that we know anything about in a short time. The dry mud around him and the hot dry air that he breathes tend to steal water out of his body, yet for some reason he doesn't dry up. In short, he goes through an endurance test that no other animal could survive.

"The second reason is that he is the closest form, among the living animals, to the extinct link between the fishes and the first land animals. That mysterious creature lies buried in some Devonian sandstone or Carboniferous bed of coal. But the lungfish, though he has changed a little in his bones and fins, is living in much the same way as did his Devonian ancestors. He shows us something of how the step from life in the water to life on the land came about. He is, as I said, like a page out of life's history."

"Do you know how that step came about?" the Padre asked.

"A little. Certainly the first step in the direction of

land life was the respiration of air instead of, or in addition to, water. This important step was taken by the fishes long before fins were converted into legs with which to crawl about on land. Some of the earliest fishes, living far back in the Devonian Period, were air-breathers; the convergent lines of evidence from the living and dead records point to this. They had a lung, of sorts, into which they swallowed air and they were enabled by this unique organ to live in pools and rivers when the dry season came and the water disappeared or became foul with rotting animals and plants. They were able to survive when the other fishes were driven out, driven possibly back into the sea, or into the Beyond. . . . Here is really your connecting link in a bigger sense: a fine new organ, a new power that broadened the organism's way of living, increased its physical freedom, widened its margin of safety. More lowly forms endured, but they were restricted to a narrower field by the changed conditions. The evolution of air-breathing lungs marked an elevation in the stream of life; it had gotten over an obstacle, surmounted it by finding a new way of living."

"Why?"

"Why what?"

"Why did life surmount the obstacle?"

"By accident. The accident of mutation and the ultimate survival of the fittest. The nature of the rocks in which these fossil forms are buried, red and yellow sandstones devoid of organic matter, shows that they were probably laid down by torrential rivers spreading out at flood-time over vast plains. When the water subsided it left the fish trapped in pools and the pools dried out in the sun and the fish died by the thousands. Perhaps the fish lived along the river banks and in shallow lakes that periodically became dry in the long arid seasons between the rains. In any case it is more than probable that they lived, as the lungfish does today, in a world that pressed in upon them, that required adjustment. Not only of the individual but of the race. Out of innumerable variations, theirs were the only ones which worked. By accident, they had achieved a new way of living. These straggling survivors, when they rise to the surface of the water to fill their lungs with air, are, in a way, recapitulating the life history of the race written back in the Devonian plains when it was fighting to survive.

"When I went to Africa after these fish it was like going back four hundred million years. Only it was shorter, easier."

The Padre had pulled himself into a position of attention, and was puffing steadily on his cigar while he watched Joel's face.

"Tell me how you got them," he said.

Joel went back to his chair and sat down with his hands between his knees.

"There was nothing spectacular about it, except that the job was of a rather special nature. I wanted to do a lot of chemical work on their blood and tissues, to determine what happened to them while they were asleep in the mud. I wanted to do some experiments with them, to test their kidneys, to compare them with other animals and particularly with ourselves. It was not enough for me to have two or three—I needed dozens of them, some active, some asleep in the mud, asleep one month, three months, six months if possible.

"Of course I had to be prepared to set up a chemical laboratory in the field so I had to take with me all the reagents, the glassware, the delicate instruments that I would need. I planned everything to the last detail— went through every step of the work before I left home. I had only a limited time in which to do the job and that, naturally, made it somewhat more difficult. It was imperative not to make any mistakes.

"But the hardest part of it all was to know where to get the fish in dried mud. I knew, of course, where they had been found by others, as recorded in the surveys made by biologists in the past. But these records did not tell me whether the fish were plentiful at a particular locality or not, nor did they say much about the local conditions in regard to the dry season, the nearness and extent of the swamplands, and so on. But after going over all the records carefully and after talking to everybody who might be able to help me, I decided to go to Lake Victoria.

"So with all our scientific gear packed in our trunks we set off for Africa, prepared to step in a few weeks from the twentieth century back to the Middle Devonian Period. I really thought about the fish that way, sometimes. They lured me, fascinated me. I wondered how they lived during their long summer sleep, and what they burned for fuel; if they remembered the simple things of life, like swimming, eating, fighting; if they really slept and could be kept asleep when taken out of their mud nest. I wondered why they didn't die of auto-intoxication while they were buried for months, for years, in the hard earth without water, kidneys paralysed, blood concentrated, life at its lowest ebb. I wondered more things about them than I could have found out in a life-time, more than I had tools to measure.

"But I was prepared to find out what I could about the mystery of their life when I found my fish. That was the first job, and for it I was dependent upon such information as I could pick up after I got to Africa.

It was a case of going in the general direction of Lake Victoria and asking our way as we went, until we should find someone who had seen them and could tell us something about the local conditions, here or there.

"As a rule the average man doesn't know the scientific names of the things around him; you have to describe them, but there seemed to be little chance of confusing this fish with any other because of its peculiar life habits. We found men—coffee planters, hunters, engineers experienced in the bush—who had heard of them or seen them. One man told us how the natives dug the fish out of the mud for food; how they would go along the dried water-courses and watch for the blow-holes through which the fish gets air, and how they would push a stick down into every suspicious hole, and if it smelled of fish on withdrawal they would dig up the victim with some mud around him and take him home for safekeeping until they were ready to eat him. The Swahilis, they said, called the fish *samaki ya donga,* 'fish of the dried-up water-courses.' But nobody seemed to know just where they could be found in any abundance; it appeared that you only occasionally, *very occasionally,* ran into one. I began to have visions of spending all our time hunting for the fish instead of doing the chemical work which we had set out to do. One man would insist that we should go to Lake Rudolph, and another that we should go up the Nile into the Sudan, or over into the Belgian Congo. Everybody agreed that the rains had been unusually late and heavy and that it would be very difficult to find the fish in mud just then, anywhere. It seemed that we should have come in January, or last year or the year before. Everybody was more or less guessing, and every guess only served to increase my nervousness.

"I don't need to tell you how big Central Africa is, but you really can't appreciate its size until you start out to find something in it. It is a tremendous target—Abyssinia, Kenya, Tanganyika, Uganda, Congo, Sudan—and you need to aim where you want to land or you practically have to go back and start all over. There is no running from here to there if you have only a few months to spend—when five hundred miles may mean five weeks of *safari*. We were headed for Lake Victoria and we had to keep going in that direction. And that is where we got our fish. I know now that it is probably the best place in all Africa to get them, everything considered, but there was a time when I doubted if they occurred there at all.

"Like all big-game hunters we stopped in Nairobi to assemble our gear and to get oriented before diving into the blue. You see, as yet I didn't know whether to take fishing rods along with me, or picks and shovels.

There was a Natural History Museum in Nairobi and I felt sure that the people in charge of it would be able to put me on to the right track. So the first thing I did was to go to the Museum. I had some difficulty finding it and more difficulty getting in. It consisted of a small building, hardly larger than one good room, and it was only after some pounding and knocking about that I stirred up the keeper. This person turned out to be a ferocious-looking Masai buck; his ears were adorned with a half-pound of brass and copper pendants, and his neck was encircled by what appeared at first sight to be a string of human teeth. I thought that he was part of the collection until he took me by the arm and led me inside to an open Visitors' Book with a notice to 'Please Sign Here.' It was also part of his job to see that the visitor deposited a shilling in a box conveniently placed for that purpose. He was admirably suited to his responsibilities for I can't imagine anyone arguing with him about a shilling or anything else. I tried to find out from him who was the Director of the Museum, but in answer to my questions he only led me back to the collection box and pointed to it with a broad grin, so I gave it up as hopeless.

"Nor could I find out from anybody else. Nobody seemed to know anything about the Museum, except that you had to pay a shilling admission and that the antelope heads were not nearly so good as those you could shoot on their *shamba* any morning before breakfast. There seemed to be a general state of disinterest in the Museum and in science generally among the planters and tradespeople.

"But it seemed that I ought to find out *something* about my fish in Nairobi so I plodded around through the dust and made inquiries, asking people if they knew of a fish that breathed by means of lungs and lived in the dry mud during the hot season. At first they were very nice to me, but when they saw me a second time they gave me a queer, sympathetic look, as though they thought that I had had a touch of the sun. In fact, one man gave me a fatherly talk in the lobby of the Stanley Hotel. He began by asking me if I had a headache—said that I looked as if I did—and went on to explain how the one thing that one must look out for in Africa is sunstroke. Strangers were particularly sensitive and should keep their sun-helmets on, even when under cover. He had had a friend who had carelessly slept on his helmet and cracked it, and the poor man had fallen dead in the street two days later. He went on in this strain for about fifteen minutes. I lost interest in his pathological monologue and began to think about getting out of Nairobi and on to Lake Victoria, and about getting some gear and a few provisions. I broke in on the gentleman's dissertation on sunstroke to ask where I could buy some canned pork and beans. He told me to go to Safariland, Ltd.

"Safariland, Ltd., is a company—or a British gentleman, to be exact—that specializes in outfitting the *safaris* of big-game hunters. If you want to shoot a pair of big tuskers or to set up an African Wing in the Museum at Weehaucus, Safariland, Ltd., has just what you need. It's a clearing house for baked beans, beds, porters, guns, tents, and so on, as well as for professional hunters who know where to find any kind of game that has ever been seen in Africa. I went around to talk to the proprietor about my modest requirements.

"I told him why I had come to Africa, but he had never seen a lungfish. He said that he had lived in Nairobi for many years and that he had never even heard of it. I think he was a little offended with me when I insisted that such a thing as a lungfish lived in Africa; I admit that I felt a little bit foolish when I set my opinion against the heads and what-nots all over the walls. But he was very decent, if sceptical, and he promised to make inquiries. He gave me the impression that if it turned out that the lungfish really lived in Africa he planned to add it to his advertised list of East African Fauna and get in a stroke ahead of his competitors. He could have special rods and reels, or picks and shovels—whatever one might need for the purpose—in readiness for the next customer.

"As I was about to leave, some remark I made about the States started a new train of thought in his mind. Somebody *had* said something to him about a letter from an American, a letter asking where he could get some fish in Africa. (I had, as a matter of fact, written a letter addressed to the Director of the Natural History Museum at Nairobi, explaining my mission and requesting assistance upon my arrival.) The letter, he went on, had been turned over to the dentist chap.

"I felt a vague sense of uneasiness about the way scientific correspondence was handled in Africa. I had already become self-conscious about my problem and I suspected that people thought I was possessed by a strange obsession which they found amusing, even if pathetic. When I accosted someone to inquire my way I expected a curt 'No, I never heard of any such fish.' Even the 'ricksha boys seemed to look at me a little differently. My abjection became complete when he said that they had turned my letter over to the dentist chap. I couldn't have felt worse had he said the police!

" 'The dentist,' he went on after an interminable interval of staring at the ceiling, 'is secretary to the Kenya and Uganda Scientific Society.' Then he told me his name and where I could find him.

"I looked him up. He was a delightful man! He dentisted in the morning and in the afternoon he retired, unapproachable by any pain, to a sanctuary at the rear of his house where he had built himself a laboratory—a photographic room, a library, a museum: a museum filled, not with human teeth and bridges, but with rare exotic birds and butterflies and monstrous insects; impala, zebra, and waterbuck heads; countless strange and beautiful things out of the heart of Africa, all collected and classified with a purpose.

"Van Wernigen, his name was. I've been told that throughout the length of Kenya and Uganda, that even over in the forests of the Belgian Congo, you heard Van Wernigen's name. They say that out in the depths of the jungle you might come suddenly upon a black tearing madly through the bushes with a butterfly net in his hands, specimen-gathering for *Bwana* Van Wernigen. He went out himself frequently, and always took his vacations in the bush, leaving the Nairobi teeth to ache by themselves; up to Kampala or to the Mountains of the Moon with a string of blacks packing along boxes of pins, formaldehyde, paint brushes, wire cages, notebooks. He had painted every bird in Kenya and Uganda, male and female, in their summer and winter plumage!

"When I saw him he was engrossed in the phenomena of mimicry among butterflies. Some butterflies, you know, are not eaten by birds, monkeys, and other animals because of a malodorous or distasteful secretion; other butterflies which are edible secure protection by mimicking the inedible model in coloration and design so closely that only expert examination can detect the difference. Van Wernigen had followed out this process of mimicry within one wide-spread species which mimicked, in different parts of the country, five different inedible models. He showed me the collection of mounted butterflies which he had made to illustrate the development of the pattern in the mimic. At the centre was a primitive butterfly, and radiating from this were five lines leading to five different models, each line made up of butterflies which successively resembled their respective models more and more until the final mimic was almost impossible to distinguish from the model which it imitated. To prove that all these mimics were really one species he had bred them and raised them in captivity. To prove that the mimics really secured immunity by means of their protective colouring he tested them on monkeys. He had a red colobus chained to the front porch which he called the 'testing laboratory.' The monkey loved butterflies but when he was offered an offensive species he would turn his head to one side as much as to say, 'Don't bother me with that thing, it's not fit to eat.' He could tell at a glance that it was inedible. He would reject the mimic in the same way but he would devour its wingless body with relish. Only the appearance of the mimic protected it, you see, for it was really edible. And thus the man worked—he tested everything in nature's own laboratory, he borrowed the eyes of the jungle itself for his work. He collected in every part of Central Africa, mounted the specimens, prepared the wax models of flowers and leaves and assembled them into beautiful and realistic settings—all the time with his eyes on the living animal and its ways, on the mystery and meaning of life.

"Of course, he knew my lungfish; he knew them by their Latin names, knew where they lived and where to get them. He had once brought several of them home with him and put them into jars filled with mud and let the mud dry out. He had kept them in the hard mud for eighteen months and then watched the fish break out of the mud when the jars were immersed in water. He showed me the jaw-bones of a big lungfish and we talked about the massive teeth shaped for crushing snail-shells and bivalves. He told me that the best place to collect them was at Kisumu and he gave me introductions to the officials there that proved invaluable. He made only one mistake—he said that I would not have any trouble in getting the fish after I got to Kisumu, the natives there would collect them for me. Let me tell you, I had plenty of trouble. . . .

"But I was full of confidence when I walked out of his house, elated with success, stimulated by the man I had been talking to. I lingered to admire his garden. I would like to live in a place like that—a sort of sophisticated jungle. The house was set at the end of a long driveway lined with casuarina trees with giant sissals set in between them. Then the trees fell back around the yard which was hedged by hibiscus bushes bearing big rose-red double blossoms; the yard was cut up by rows of willowy eucalyptus trees and palms into patches of yellow asters, roses, cosmos, and a dozen other flowers. The house stood against a flamboyant in full bloom and a purple bougainvillæa spread across the entire front porch. There was colour everywhere. In every patch of sun there was some gorgeous colour, and in every patch of shade there was dark-green moss or a pale-green fern. There was some sort of little primitive mammal running around the yard, and an evil-tongued parrot scolded the colobus on the front porch. Altogether it was a delightful place. I had never seen the tropics so intimately before and the essence of their rank vitality, their differentness, seemed to be concentrated in that yard.

"Yes, and the essence of my adventure. I was well pleased with my prospects. I wanted to go back to Safariland, Ltd., and buy a substantial order of fish-nets and other gear and carry them into the Stanley Hotel over my shoulder as a symbol of my sanity. Fortunately I didn't, or the joke would have been on me. For when I finally got my fish I did not use a fish-net or even a pick and shovel to dig them out of the mud. I just picked them up off the ground."

III

J OEL accepted another cigar from the Padre and nodded his head appreciatively after lighting it.

"Another miracle?" the Padre asked, smiling and
taking a fresh cigar for himself.

"Yes, for me it was," Joel laughed, "for I ultimately
came to a point where it seemed that only a miracle
could save my little expedition from defeat.

"I supposed that the people around Mombasa and
Nairobi had never heard of the lungfish because the
animal did not occur in their immediate neighbourhood.
But when I got to Kisumu, where I knew on good
authority that the lungfish did occur, I did not find my
informants much more helpful. Of course, the proper
thing was to go to the natives for information, especially
since I hoped to rely largely upon them for collecting
the fish for me. But it was several days before the
P.C., who was acting as interpreter for me, could collect
the head men for the necessary *shauri*. Meanwhile, the
people of Kisumu took us in hospitably and gave us
an empty cottage to live in and to use as a laboratory,

and they elected us to a temporary membership in the local Club.

"The industry of your British colonist is remarkable: wherever you find two or more Englishmen gathered together, there you will find a golf course, a tennis court, and one or more clubhouses. The Nyanza Club at Kisumu is a beautiful place, high up on a hill which overlooks the Kavirondo Gulf at the eastern end of Lake Victoria. The hill slopes gently down to the Lake and is dotted here and there with thorn trees, euphorbias, and low bushes. A wide drive lined with gum trees and casuarinas runs along the shore for some distance and then it doubles back along the crest of the hill and into the town proper. Our cottage was almost the last one out of town near the end of the hill where the road doubles back from the Lake. It was surrounded by frangipani bushes in full bloom, an occasional pink trumpet flower, and wiry euphorbias. From the front yard you looked down the open slope of the hill to the Lake and across to the blue mountains behind Homa Bay. The men at the Club used to joke about being in the Heart of Darkest Africa, but the term sounded absurd when you saw the *Clement Hill* come steaming in from Jinja or when you heard the train whistle from the railway station. The place had its African colour, however; herds of impala came to graze in the short grass around the cottage and crocodiles and hippos were common enough down in the Lake. The hippos trampled down the gardens during the night, searching for lettuce and other tender delicacies. So persistent was the hungry beast in its depredations of the Club's garden that they called him Horace and elected him to Honorary Membership. You frequently encountered Horace while driving along the Lake shore after dark, but you timed your meeting so as not to hurry him across the road; and if you chanced to find a strange, dark object in your *shamba* at night you waved your arms—if it was Horace, he went away. Horace was immune from attack because you simply can't kill a three-ton hippo in a settled community—it is too difficult to shift camp!

"Oh, no! In spite of the steamship and the railway and motor cars we didn't forget that we were in Africa, especially at night. We were far out from the town proper, and after our boys had gone home the fun began. The hyenas prowled around the back porch, knocking over pots and pans, and Horace ambled around in the darkness and sneezed that sneeze of his which sounds like nothing so much as a steam-boiler blowing out its insides; and other nocturnal visitors found ways and means of making strange and unearthly noises right under our windows. If they had only blown that train whistle about nine o'clock **at** night it would have helped a lot!

"But to come back to the fish. As I said, nobody there seemed to know much about it. They were, of course, very interested and I had to tell them all about the fish while we sat in the Club, how it buried itself in the mud and breathed air, and so on, while we drank each other's health and the success of the expedition. The Club was one of these progressive clubs—each newcomer buys a drink for everybody who is already there and this keeps up until nobody else comes and everybody decides that it's time to go home. If there were many late-comers you might not get home until eleven, but the local cooks were used to this regime and had dinner ready at any hour up to midnight. I used to wonder if they didn't do most of their own sleeping between tea and dinner-time.

"Late in the course of our first evening at the Club the engineer in charge of the P.W.D. came in. He spent most of his time in the bush, building bridges and roads and he said that he had frequently heard of the lungfish and knew just where he could get them, although he had never actually seen one. His information, **as is** frequently the case with a layman, appeared to be a bit sketchy but I thought it important to follow up **every** lead. He said that he knew where he could dig **one or** more out of the mud and he suggested that we go after them the next day. Of course I was enthusiastic, so we began to make plans and talked about them most of the evening. He wanted to make an early start. He had *jembies* for digging, but he said that we would need some sort of trap to catch the fish in because when it was unearthed it wriggled away over the ground with great rapidity. We finally decided to borrow a washtub from the steward and some string and so on, and planned to rig up a trap in the field. I was feeling pretty cheerful. Old P.W.D. explained again how you located the place where the fish was buried by spotting the blow-holes which could be seen frequently alongside, or even in the middle of the muddy roads.

" 'And you'd be surprised,' he said, 'how those fish love air. I've had four punctures in a week from fish coming up and biting my automobile tires to get at it!'

"Only then did I realize that he had never seen a lungfish's hole. I had a feeling like falling through space, but I suppose I made some sort of smiling grimace to show my appreciation of the joke.

"But the next day the P.C. got the natives together for a big *shauri*. As soon as he explained to them what I wanted they spoke up and said that they knew the fish. They described it fairly well—as well as you can roughly describe any fish—and said that it buried itself in the mud during the dry season. That was the fish I wanted, I said. They went on to tell how it had 'whiskers' around its mouth by which it suckled its young. I remember how the P.C. wrinkled his forehead and looked up at me at this bit of natural history, but I suggested that we might take a look at this fish, anyway. The description seemed to fit the lungfish in every respect except the whiskers part of it, and these I took to be a misinterpretation of the lungfish's rope-like, pectoral fins. So we told the boys to bring us in one of their fish, and the next day I was all primed to have my first lungfish.

"But the fish turned out to be a common catfish, hence the whiskers. The natives were right about the catfish burying itself in the mud, but it is not a lungfish. It aerates its blood by means of a spongy tissue rich in capillaries in the mouth—a relatively recent device—and it was not of immediate interest to me.

"So we tried again, getting natives in from all around the neighbouring country. At last we got on to what I felt sure was spoor: it was described as a big fish that slept in the mud and had two rope-like arms in front by which it suckled its young. (The P.C. began to shy away at this, but I held him on.) It was a cross between a fish and a crocodile and there were no females; the father laid the eggs. The fish was called Kamongo. It was a very fierce fish and it would bite you if you came near it. It would even bite you two days after you had cut its head off. 'The *Bwana* must not go near the fish until it was dead,' they said. The P.C. remarked that if I had to wait until two days after the fish died I couldn't work in Kisumu—the Health Officer would object!

"All this was very well, but where could we get this fierce fish?

" 'The *Bwana* can't get it,' they said, 'he has come at the wrong time! The *dongas* are all under water. The *Bwana* must come back in December.'

"That the *dongas* were all under water was clear enough by that time. The rains had been unusually prolonged and, what was more important, Lake Victoria was at the highest point that it had reached for years. There is a cycle in the level of Lake Victoria which runs over a period of about eleven years—it appears to be tied up somehow with sunspots—which shows up in the local water levels far back from the Lake itself. But I didn't know anything about this until I got over there on the ground. Here I ran into serious trouble for the mud was certainly under water, knee-deep, and there wasn't a chance in a million of my finding a lungfish that had been dried out for even a short period of time. Had those beggars really known they could have told me to come back in five years, at which time I could find vast swamps hard and cracked by the torrid sun that in two or six months might just be emerging from their present flood.

"Since I couldn't wait for the Nile to drain Lake Victoria, I had to give up all immediate hope of studying the fish in æstivation. The best I could do was to make what observations I could on the free-swimming fish, and to try to take some home alive. If I could get them back alive perhaps I could do what Van Wernigen had done, put them into mud and dry them out artificially, so to speak. The plan had its advantages: with the fish once asleep in my laboratory I could control the conditions of their life, such as temperature, humidity, and so on, and I could make more leisurely and refined observations upon them than I could ever hope to make in the field.

"But I had still to get the fish. As yet, I had never seen one.

" 'Where does the fish go,' I asked, 'when the *dongas* are under water?'

"They had several answers to this: one man said that the fish dissolved and was washed away, and another suggested that it dug itself deeper into the mud, but a third and really bright boy pointed out that if I could use a dead fish I could get it at the fish-market.

"Following this pregnant suggestion I inquired at the fish-market and found that Kamongo was occasionally caught by the fishermen at Nanga, a village about five miles along the Lake. It was a hot day, but I went over there that very afternoon with an interpreter to see if I could get them to direct their energies in my behalf.

"They admitted that they caught Kamongo once in a while, but they said that they could not bring them in alive because, in the first place, the fish were very dangerous and had to be killed at once by a blow over the head; and in the second place, if they didn't kill them they would die anyway in a short time! I suggested that I might come out with them and take the fish out of the nets myself. Yes, I could take the fish out of the nets if I wanted to, but I'd never get them back to the shore alive; they wouldn't live after they had been taken out of the water more than a few hours. I said that I would bring a *mtungi* to put water in, and put the fish in the water and take it back to the shore that way. They shook their heads: No, it would die more quickly in a *mtungi* than anywhere else. A Kamongo was the most delicate of all fish and died at once when it was caught. I would either have to use dead Kamongo or else I would have to use some other kind of fish that could be kept alive. This seemed to me to be very strange, but I decided to try my luck with the fish-nets anyway, and promised them a handsome price (as judged by local fish prices) for every Kamongo that I took from them. I arranged to meet them at the place in the Lake where their nets were set at about three o'clock the following morning.

"At last I had come to the end of my trail! All I had to do was to go out in a motor boat in the early hours and take the fish out of the fishermen's nets, put them into tubs or *mtungis* filled with water and bring them in alive to the laboratory. The next morning saw me puff-puffing across the lake toward my rendezvous with the fishermen and my first live lungfish—or so I thought.

"As I went along I mused on the workings of the native mind. I could see why they believed the lungfish suckled its young by the two pectoral appendages which were, in spite of their rope-like character, quite obviously fins. And I was beginning to understand why they thought that the animal was a cross between a fish and a crocodile; the more I heard of Kamongo's character the more I appreciated their descriptive, if unbiological, blending. The astonishing statement that there was no female fish I attributed to the peculiar familial arrangements of the lungfish; the female lays the eggs and then wanders off to more engaging pastimes while the male stays behind and guards the nest. If the water becomes foul, he even stirs himself to the extent of beating it up with his tail to aerate it. I suppose that when the young grow up and are about to leave the nest the old boy eats most of them as a reward for duty faithfully done. Many fish consider this fair play, and Kamongo is a frightful cannibal, anyway—he will eat his aquarium mates if he gets hungry. The business of biting you for two days after decapitation, I learned later, was merely an exaggeration. The head, when severed from the body, will snap reflexly for some time and frequently displays rather horrifying gasps of asphyxiation. But that the fish would not live in a tub of water I knew to be an absurdity, for couldn't it live for a year out of water entirely? It certainly wasn't going to die in a tub of water in a couple of hours! The natives had probably just jumped to conclusions in this matter from observing how quickly other fishes die in a limited volume of water.

"But do you know that they were right? I'm blessed if I didn't come to think that those fish were being guarded by some African Malignity determined to keep them from me. Every fish which I took out of those nets kicked about in my tubs for a half-hour or so and then rolled over on its back and died. Some of them even died in my trembling fingers as I disentangled the net from around their squirming bodies! Even the most perfect specimens, without a scratch on them, went the same way! I tell you that I began to be frightened!

Frightened by the absurd possibility that I had come ten thousand miles only to look down at those slimy carcasses of dead fish; frightened by the apparent impossibility of ever getting them back alive to America.

"Yes, it was absurd; but the genuineness of my panic comes back to me now as I see myself marching determinedly down to the Lake at the next midnight to try again, my way lighted by a flickering kerosene lantern. I barely noticed the hippos that moved in the bushes along the road or the hyenas that skitted out of my path. I believe that I would have passed a lion face to face with indifference, so great was my absorption in my difficulty. I was certainly possessed by a monomania now. Perhaps it was the intensity of my possession that blinded me to the explanation of my difficulty. But it was as simple as I was blind!

"The word had gone out that I wanted Kamongo, and that I would pay a handsome price to anybody who would bring them to me alive. A few fish had been brought to the cottage by various natives, but they had invariably died within a few hours after I had got them. This thing was getting serious, and I was all the more perturbed because it seemed so senseless. I could not reconcile this extreme delicacy with the fact that the fish could live for months in the dry mud. The more

I thought about it the more absurd the whole thing became.

"I sat on the front steps with my chin in my hands wondering in a dazed sort of way just what I was going to do next. There didn't seem to be anything to do, except to go back over my same old tracks and try it again. It was the most helpless feeling I've ever had. I saw myself going home and reporting that there seemed to be plenty of lungfish in Lake Victoria but that you couldn't get them out alive—they died as soon as you looked at them, died of fright, or of some mysterious kind of piscine heart-failure. I was sitting there mooning, with my eyes fixed on the mountains across the Kavirondo Gulf, when my houseboy came tearing up the hill excited with news that he knew would bring me to my feet.

" '*Bwana,* Oworogwada comes! He brings Kamongo, live Kamongo!'

"Oworogwada was a native chief with whom I had held several *shauris.* I got up to look and sure enough the old chief himself was coming leisurely up the grassy slope of the hill. He was dressed in an orange nightgown and he was pulling steadily on a black clay pipe. Even at some distance I could see that he had on all his ceremonial teeth and bones, and that his ears were fringed from top to bottom with the malachite pendants of magic. Clearly, this was a notable occasion! But I didn't see any Kamongo.

"The old man was followed by his eldest son, a strapping buck of thirty-odd who was chewing on the end of some dentifricial root. Bringing up the rear was a grandson, age ten years or thereabouts, with nothing on his body; but on his head was a *mtungi* at least two feet across. In due time the Kamongo was disclosed curled up inside the *mtungi* in about eight inches of water. The fish was nearly five feet long and, with the *mtungi* and water, must have weighed as much as its porter.

"Oworogwada explained that he had found a nest in the swamplands and trapped the fellow in a big *basketi*. The job had taken him a couple of days, and of course he was quite set up by his ingenuity and success.

"No less than I. You can imagine my elation! I made haste to transfer the fish to a tub filled with fresh water. I cautiously placed my hands around the massive throat and lifted out my prize, the slime running down off its black body on to my legs and feet. But the beast's mouth was open wide in a terrifying, final gasp! It was rigid with *rigor mortis!*

"As I looked into its gaping maw I broke out in a delirious shout of laughter. I saw at last my own absurdity. The fish had *drowned,* of course! They had drowned in the fishermen's nets, in the shallow tubs, they had drowned on me right and left because they could not get to the precious air. Lungfish indeed! Drowned beneath the water!

"I have to laugh now when I wonder what the old chief thought of my unexpected reaction. Admittedly these *Bwanas* were strange fellows, always making absurd demands. But my explosion into laughter, coupled with his own consternation at finding the fish dead, must certainly have puzzled him.

"I gave him two shillings for his trouble and I told him to bring me the next one in an old gunny sack which I gave him for the purpose. This request must have seemed to him like outright insanity but he pocketed the shillings and went away in stately procession, followed by the royal heirs.

"Looking back in the light of subsequent discoveries, I wonder that it did not occur to me sooner that these creatures might be entirely dependent upon aerial respiration. As a matter of fact, they cannot live beneath the water for more than a few hours. Their gills are greatly reduced in size, almost vestigial, and even in the water they rise to the surface every fifteen minutes or so to fill their lungs with air. To reach the surface they must be able to bend the forward part of their long bodies, and this had been impossible in the narrow tubs in which the fishermen had put them—if they were not already drowned by being imprisoned in the net below the surface of the water for an indefinite period of time. It's clear enough now, but sometimes we are a long time seeing simple things.

"But the mere explanation of my difficulties did not solve them for me. I still had to find a way to catch the fish without drowning them and, it was clear, I must confine myself to small fish not over a foot or so in length that could move about freely in the tubs and buckets which were all I had to keep them in. Such small fish are not caught by the fishermen's nets because they can slip through the meshes. We had tried a hook and line at several places on the Lake, but without success. We had no fine mesh drag-nets, and it would have taken weeks to make them. The peculiar nature of the fish I wanted rendered useless the local fishing methods, so far as getting them alive was concerned; and in the heart of Africa you can't go out and buy something else when what you have doesn't work. No, it didn't look so easy. But, as it happened, all my difficulties were solved for me at once, and in a most peculiar fashion.

"The cottage in which we were living had, up to a few days before our arrival, been occupied by the Superintendent of the Prison who had vacated it to move into newly completed quarters. I had never met the man but he had often been in my mind because each morning a gang of convicts would pass by our door on the way to the shore where they were cutting out papyrus. The average black looks awesome enough to a new-comer, but thirty or more strapping bucks already convicted of criminal tendencies and guarded only by one or two *askaris* are a sight to instill trepidation. The guard seemed to me to be too light. I could watch the prisoners working on the shore from our front porch; armed with big knives, *jembies,* and ropes they would walk out on to the islands of papyrus that had blown in from across the Gulf and cut off the feathery tops. Then they would cut out big blocks of roots and, working a rope around them, pull them ashore where they burned them. The *askaris* were armed, of course, but they sauntered around in a casual sort of way and I rather looked forward to their getting the job done and moving away from our front yard.

"On the afternoon of the very day that Oworogwada visited us I received a message asking me to come over to the Prison. I must have looked rather haggard when I got there. I had been losing a lot of good sleep collecting dead fish from the Lake, and what with the hot sun and the dust of my walk and with my worrying generally about the thing all the way over I wasn't in any too cheerful a mood. The Superintendent didn't immediately improve it.

"He started off by saying how sorry he was that I couldn't get what I'd come after. The water, he said, was over his cabbage patch and that was very unusual. He suggested that I try such and such a *donga,* that it was usually dry this time of year. But it happened that I had already tried such and such a *donga* and had found the water even deeper than over his precious cabbage patch. He ventured that if I could wait a couple of months his cabbage patch would be dry; he was certain that there were lungfishes in it because he had seen the boys digging there. I said that I was sorry but I could not wait a couple of months, for I had to be back in America by the first of October. I hoped his cabbages were not ruined by the flood, however. Oh, not likely— they would come along sooner or later. Cabbages grew almost any time in Africa—not that they ever got to be cabbages, properly speaking, not like the cabbages you get at home. . . . But what was I going to do about the lungfish?

"I told him that I had given up all hope of getting the fish out of dry mud, and that I was trying now to get some small ones alive to take home with me.

"He turned to me with a surprised look and asked: 'Why don't you go and pick some up?'

"For a moment my sight was obscured by the vision of a lungfish biting an automobile tire.

" 'Do I need a washtub?' I finally asked him.

" 'Oh, no,' he answered, 'come along.'

"I decided to take a chance. I followed him into his car and we drove back past the cottage and down to the Lake shore where the labour gang was working. He called something in Swahili to a guard and the man brought him a galvanized iron bucket which he passed on to me.

"In it were a half-dozen live lungfish, kicking around as happy as larks.

" 'They fall out,' he explained, 'when the boys drag the papyrus roots ashore. They usually keep them for dinner but if you want them I'll have them put on your porch. It's funny, isn't it?' he went on; 'I just threw away a barrel of fifty of them when I moved out of the bungalow. My son had kept them there all winter. I'll tell the *askaris* to save them for you tomorrow—'

" 'Thanks,' I said, 'and I'll take these now!'

"I took them back to the cottage and went to work on them. Within a month I had collected all the lungfish that I wanted, picked them up literally in my own front yard! The Superintendent kindly kept the labour gang cutting papyrus long after it was really necessary. In fact, I think that he rounded up a few islands just for

my special benefit. I remember that man most kindly.
I do hope that he had a good crop of cabbages. . . .

"It wasn't a very sporting method of fishing but it
served the ends of science. . . .

"Oh, yes, I got them to America all right—carried
them all the way out of Kenya, through the Red Sea and
across the Atlantic without a single casualty; took them
to a modern laboratory and put them to sleep in glass
jars, in American mud in which their ancestors had
slept countless generations ago. They went to sleep in
an incubator which was tenderly guarded by a thermo-
stat and surrounded by test-tubes, gas-analysers, burettes,
and colorimeters, just as comfortably as in the Karno
plains, unconscious of the change in scenery . . . unconscious that they were part of an experiment. . . ."

"Was your experiment a success?" The Padre asked
when Joel gave no sign of going on.

Joel laughed. "Oh, I wasn't thinking so much about
my experiment. I was really thinking about Nature's
experiment, performed four hundred million years ago
when the first Kamongo dug into the mud to avoid
desiccation on some arid Devonian plain. My job was
merely to watch Nature's experiment and to record the
results in my note-book, to observe what life does when
it is crowded too near the edge."

"Well, was that experiment a success?"

Joel laughed again, and getting stiffly out of his chair he began to pace up and down the deck with his hands behind him, while his eyes were studying the white dowelled planks beneath his feet.

"In so far as we can see those things, I wouldn't say that it was. He buried himself in the mud, you see, and for most purposes that rather put an end to things. He shut himself up in a prison from which escape hung upon the slenderest thread of accident—that the waters should rise again before he reached the end of his rope. He shut himself up where he had to burn his own tissues for fuel to keep the spark of life in his body; if he didn't die of starvation then the chances were that he would be killed by desiccation when the mud dried too far and cracked open his water-proof nest. If he escaped these hazards he had to go forth on the newly arrived flood and seek food and face his enemies in an emaciated condition, debilitated rather than rested by his long sleep. In any case, he traded safety beneath the water for safety in that marginal zone where water meets the land.

"No—when he dived into the mud he dived into a blind alley, into a mode of life that must ultimately end in extinction. The proof of my reasoning lies in the fact that he is nearing that end. The marvel is that he has survived this long. His failure is the more pathetic since his was such a clever start. This lung of his, which promised to bring him freedom from the old way of living, promised to break the bonds that chained him to a life beneath the water, but it only left him chained alternately beneath the water and the mud. If anything, he was worse off than before.

"In addition to the air-breathing lung, he needed legs to crawl about with, to take him out of the dried-up water-courses and over the land to some place where the water was still standing. His own fins were too feeble, too piscine, for that purpose.

"The legs came, but not to the lungfish; they came to some air-breathing cousin of his who had stronger bones and muscles in his fins, better raw materials. Can you see the scene: a desiccating swampland where Cousin, with his primitive stumps of fin-legs, raises himself out of the hardening mud, laboriously climbs up the bank, and crawls away to some distant green oasis and to freedom—without once looking back at my poor lungfish, left wallowing helplessly behind, getting ready to dive into his sticky prison, his blind alley?

"Cousin is gone; we have nothing but his footprints—where he walked along the mud which the sun baked hard and the wind covered over—to tell the tale of that experiment. But through him life escaped out of that treacherous swamp to crawl about on land, escaped to a bigger and better way of living, to a greater degree of physical freedom. It escaped to an open road which led on and on. Yes, Cousin was a very successful experiment!

"But my lungfish bound himself down to a narrower way of living, he reduced his physical freedom when he dived into the mud; he got into a way of living that had no future, into a blind alley. He was an experiment that failed."

Joel took a couple of turns around the cramped deck and then he stopped, half-facing the Padre.

"It's clear enough to us now, when we are looking back upon it, but I wonder, if we had been there half suffocated in that black mud, could we have told which was the blind and which was the open road? . . . I doubt it."

He went off again into his deliberate pacing up and down.

IV

IT was the Padre's turn to become infected with the restlessness that kept Joel moving, and he began to follow his companion around, looking intently at Joel's heels as though he were playing some inane game of stepping in his predecessor's footsteps. Joel stopped to kick a deck-chair out of his path and this let the Padre come abreast with him. The latter gave the chair another push, and then the two men started off in step. The free space was limited, however, by recumbent sleepers who blocked their way, and after a few cramped turns the Padre suggested that they go forward to the bow. "I like the sharp end of a boat," he said; "it gives me an illusion of grandeur." So they moved off in the half-shadows, carefully stepping over the outstretched legs and up-turned feet of their fellow-passengers.

The stairway that led down to the forward well-deck presented some difficulty. At its top was one of those gates which by its very nature is supposed to restrain ambitious vagrants: a gate patterned, like the ship's rail, of horizontal iron bars let into somewhat heavier uprights, the

whole slung from four protruding hooks which fitted
into rings upon the rail-posts. To pass by, you had to lift
the gate up and out of the holding-rings and then you
were faced with the problem of knowing what to do
with it, for you must neither take it along with you or
else do a sharp turn on the narrow topmost step of the
ladder and put it back into its place—which was almost
an impossibility. To lay hands upon such a gate made
you unpleasantly aware that you were a trespasser. After
several attempts to open it, they were forced to climb over
the rail and worm themselves on to the steps of the steep
ladder.

The forward hatch had been uncovered, preparatory
to unloading cargo at Port Saïd, and the hatch-boards
and tarpaulins were piled in rows along the bulwarks.
The intervening deck-space was littered with gear and
sleeping sailors, and the men had to pick their way carefully to the forecastle through a confusion of shadows.
Another steep ladder led up to the forecastle-deck; here
they stumbled over steam-pipes and anchor-chains until
at last they came into the bow. Three steps ascended
from the forecastle-deck to a shallow bracket set into the
bow; the bracket afforded a comfortable place to stand
or sit, and it was sheltered by the bulwarks where they
rose high above the hawse-pipes so that by leaning over
one could look down at the prow cutting through the

black water. A large searchlight fixed upon the bow il-luminated the sides of the canal and the water ahead.

The ship was just turning through the curve of Lake Timsah, and the lights of Ismaïlia sparkled on the west. She seemed to be making greater speed in the open water and her bow moved up and down with a slight but exuberant motion. The stars, instead of sliding from side to side as they do when viewed from a rolling ship, appeared to rise and fall like a canopy fitfully inflated by the wind. The illusion was emphasized by the reflection from the water of the searchlight, the radiance of which was alternately concentrated and scattered by a low procession of rounded waves.

Leaning over the bulwark it seemed to Joel that he was looking down upon a pit in the bottom of which a moving stream of water was splitting itself against a rock. There was nothing along the vertical prow to give it its proper dimensions. It was hard to believe that just below Cape Guardafui seas had swept across that bow and shattered themselves against the windlasses and ventilators behind. But out there in the Indian Ocean the monsoon had had three thousand miles of fairway in which to stir the water up, while here there was only a small lake and a little wisp from some Ægean gale that, having spent itself on the broad Mediterranean, now swung eastward to die above the Desert of Arabia.

"I wish that were Port Saïd," Joel said.

The Padre did not answer him. His back was turned to Joel, and the latter fell to musing on the freedom that now lay but a few hours ahead. He was anxious to stretch his legs on land after his long imprisonment. He had visions of himself climbing down the ship's ladder into an Arab boat, climbing out upon the float and up the steps at the landing wharf. He saw himself going through the streets, still brightly lighted by the open shops and cafés in spite of the late hour, pushing off the importunate guides and pedlars as he found his way to a table on the sidewalk.

Curious beggars, those pedlars, they never seemed to sleep. They were always on the spot whenever a ship came in, any hour of the day or night. They boarded her before the anchor was down, swarming up her sides on grappling poles for all the world like a band of bloody pirates. They pushed into every recess and sat squat-legged on the deck while they spread out their wares in a neat array: all the junk in the world—picture postcards, glass beads, amber beads, stone beads, Turkish paste ("good for the stomach, mister!"), ivory elephants in a procession of grandfather to great-grandson—all the junk in the world, half of it made in Birmingham or Manchester and all of it priced at ten times its real value (if any). But all of it, the bustle and noise and confusion, was fascinating with novelty. It beat upon the senses with the refreshing vigour of a showerbath! If the robbers didn't get your money on the ship there was another horde waiting to pester you when you stepped ashore, or to hover near your table on the sidewalk trying to engage you in a bartering contest.

And the dirty little Arab tricksters with their abra-cadabra of "gilly-gilly-gilly"; for twopence they'll "gilly-gilly" a baby chick or a tumbler of water out of a mysterious nowhere, and for a shilling they will "gilly-gilly" snakes or coloured balls in and out of boxes for half an hour, while you sit at a table on the sidewalk in the early morning hours and drink long, cold drinks of lime and gin, encouraging your thirst with peanuts, chips, cheese, sandwiches—you and the tourist from Oklahoma and the diamond merchant from Antwerp and the dancing-girl from Paris and the Russian outcast and the P.C. going home on leave—while the polyglot of Saïd dins in your ears. Saïd—where every beggar in the streets is a facile linguist and every coin in the world is legal tender —where the ships of the East pause for a few short hours to coal or oil, and pay their Suez Canal fees.

The residents of Port Saïd walk up and down the breakwater past M. de Lesseps' statue and watch the ships go by. They pride themselves on being able to identify the funnel-markings on every steamship line in the world and to name its nationality. The last is not so difficult since more than fifty per cent of them fly the Union Jack. The big and little ships come and go like blood corpuscles carrying the raw materials to feed a thousand industries, or their finished products to be metabolized by a civilized world; ships from Japan with silk, pottery, matches, toys; and from China with eggs, beans, millet, cotton, peanuts, more silk, and firecrackers; from Singapore and Penang with rubber, tin, copra, gums, and rice; and from Siam and Burma with teakwood with which to build more ships; from Colombo and Bombay with tea, coconut oil, jute, cotton, gunnycloth, opium, and mail for the people back home; from Java and Sumatra with sugar, rubber, rice, and oil; and from South and East Africa with corn, wool, hides, diamonds, gold, ivory, sisal, cloves, and more coffee and tea—and back again laden with steel, machinery, railway engines, bicycles, automobiles, gramophones, cinema films, chemicals, high explosives, aeroplanes, guns; all the commerce between a billion people in the awakening East and a half-billion in mechanical Europe; between a restless, overcrowded East, eager to learn new ways, and an overcrowded Europe, eager to teach.

Thirty million tons of ships pass through the Canal each year, and more than half of them sail under one flag. In fact, more than half the ships of the world sail under that flag, and nine-tenths of these move under the ægis of two men who play them against each other like the pieces of a gigantic game of draughts. . . . M. de Lesseps was almost as far from seeing the consequences of his digging in the sand as was old King Necho who started the first canal four thousand years ago.

And the digging was far from finished, Joel noticed from an occasional suction-dredge along the bank. Here and there a track had been laid down so that the sand could be pulled by patient donkeys back into the desert. It was clear that the digging would never be over until the sand stopped blowing.

Joel tried to make out the hills where they rolled away into the desert on either side, but all that he could decipher were the outlines of those close to the shore. He gave it up with a shrug, thinking that they all looked alike anyway—a desolate monotony of shifting sand. Sand so fine that you have to look closely to see the minute black and white and red grains of it. It is stirred up by the wind and peppered against your face or twirled into whirling dervishes that skim joyously across the desert. It is piled up around your ankles in flowing stream-lines when you watch it, and when the wind is through with it, it is left in little ripples and big waves marching across the open spaces or in smooth, rounded hills, crescent-shaped as though their lee-sides had been scooped out with a big tablespoon. When the wind is through with it there are buried beneath it things which may never see the light again, plants and animals and the works of man. You can push your hand down into its soft substance to the elbow, to the shoulder, and not find the bottom. . . .

But the sand had not always been there—only recently a vast sea had covered this very land. The sea bottom had risen slowly until the Red Sea was separated from the Mediterranean; and the River Nile, carrying mud from the highlands of Abyssinia, had built out its great Delta to make the land of Egypt. The new land had become covered with a green forest of cycads, giant ferns, and equisetums, and peopled by bizarre animals; the steam-shovels while digging the Canal had unearthed their bones as they had fallen where they died, long before the sand had come. The sand was only a mantle of dust that had settled upon the earth during a quiet moment; upon an earth so sensitive that it sinks and rises with every tide or heavy rain, an earth so big that wrinkles upon its crust relatively less than the lines upon an orange could plunge the peak of Everest as far below the water as the deepest oceanic depth; an earth so restless that, in its ups and downs, cycle after cycle of life had swept across it—first below the sea for corals, worms, and trilobites and then above the sea for giant ferns and scorpions; then down again for armoured fishes and more worms and feathery sea-stars, then up for cryptogamous trees and reptiles—or perhaps only to be desert for a time before it plunged below the sea again. The broken, jagged hills, formed where the faulted crust pushed up through the Arabian sand, showed the record of that restlessness in layer after layer of limestones, sandstones, coal-beds, clays, marls, shales; if all the layers which have been washed away by wind and rain were still in place they would stand, perhaps, higher than the Himalayas. While the River Nile, which has flowed throughout the Time of Man, has laid down a mere hundred feet of mud. . . . Now the sand lay like a mantle over this buried past, covering alike the tracks of prehistoric monsters and the deserted temples of man. Man—who was always trying to conquer Nature, as though that were possible. He had dug a half-dozen canals in this very sand and, sooner or later, Nature had filled them up again. In the great panorama of time, permanence was but little more assured to man than to his footprints in the dust of that desert. . . .

Would he, Joel wondered, turn out to be a blind alley, too? The human species had already so overpopulated the earth that competition and jealousy among its own

numbers had led it to devise better and better means of
self-destruction. Would its rapid evolution be accom-
panied by an equally rapid descent and extinction? Perhaps, and then the sand could blow back leisurely and
cover the iron and mortar even as it had covered the stone
temples of four thousand years ago—and, beneath them,
the forests and swamps of prehistoric times.

————————————— V —————————————

A SUDDEN movement by the Padre made Joel look up. The Padre sat down cross-legged on the floor, resting his back against the bulwark.

"What's the matter, are you cold?" Joel asked him.

"No, no, I'm not cold. . . . Look here, I'm not satisfied with that explanation you put on your lungfish. You called him an experiment that failed, a blind alley. Don't you think you are doing him an injustice?"

Joel did not know what to say, so he put his hands in his pockets, wrinkled his brows, and stared at his feet.

"What I mean is, I don't like this blind alley sort of thing. I don't care about your lungfish—I never heard of him until you told me about him—but he seems to stand for a lot, doesn't he?

"I liked him immensely when you told me how he or his ancestors had been choked in the stagnant pools when the water dried up, and how through him life invented a new way of living, which widened its scope and increased its possibilities, by breathing air instead of water. He was magnificent then, a pioneer through

80

which life had escaped from a threatening difficulty. But dash it all, man, when you leave him behind in the mud, when you call him a futile experiment, it seems like outright desertion! Doesn't he deserve something better than that?"

Joel laughed—not that he meant to give the Padre offence, but he began to see what was bothering him, to sense his perplexity over a Nature that could play such scurvy tricks.

"It means a great deal to me. I'm lost in seeing just how he fits into my scheme of things. I must interpret him—your lungfish wallowing in the mud—and I don't like to see him called a futile experiment."

The Padre's expression, "I'm lost," brought back to Joel's mind another occasion when he had used the same words. It had been on an evening just out of Mombasa when they had been talking about the stars, the galaxies of stars that swing through the heavens at incomprehensible distances and incomprehensible speeds. "I get lost," he had said, "when I think of the magnitude of creation."

And there had been yet another time when Joel had lent him a recent best-seller. He had sat all day with his eyes glued to the pages of the novel, absorbed in its tale of passionate though unconventional love. He had handed it back with a smiling shake of his head and

some cryptic remark about "modern moral confusion."
Had he been lost in an emotional conflict stirred up by
the book's carnal realism? . . . "Glad, happy places"—
there it was again. Joel was beginning to suspect that
after five years of Africa this man, who must have set
out with such a high purpose, was beginning to chal-
lenge its wisdom. It seemed to Joel that his expression
was more than rhetorical; it spoke of a doubt nibbling
away at the roots of his faith in himself, in the universe,
in the Ultimate Goodness of Things.

Now he was saying: "Evolution has always appealed
to me. I can't understand why some people are thrown
into such a panic about it. The Church, of course, being
conservative, would stave it off as long as possible just
as the medieval churchmen fought off the newer knowledge of astronomy. But we are not so near-sighted today.
Anyway, to me this picture of life coming up to difficulties and surmounting them is magnificent! If the
old Biblical poets had had the facts that we have they
would have made equally magnificent poetry about
them. But, somehow, it doesn't seem right to mar its
magnificent character by putting in futile mistakes and
deserting the failures, now does it?"

"It may mar its magnificence for you, Padre, but it is
a cold, hard fact. My lungfish is not the only mistake
that has been made in evolution. The road is littered with

them. I think that perhaps you see evolution as a concerted movement on the part of life toward some exalted and predetermined goal, some far-off crowning pinnacle. But all the evidence is against such a view."

"Then why evolution?"

"Evolution is just a process. It simply follows a haphazard course more or less directed by its mutation and environment. The progressive idea is an illusion that comes from looking at only one part of life's history, and chiefly from our point of view. The only time when we can properly speak of evolution as being upward is in those instances where the theatre of life's activity has been enlarged, where some new acquisition or way of living permits the animal to move about more freely and independently within its environment. The evolution of lungs was upward, and so was the evolution of legs with which to crawl about the land and of wings with which to fly, and of warm-bloodedness to keep the animal warm and active throughout the winter. But all of these changes are upward only in relation to the particular time and conditions of life under which the animals which shared them lived. They are not always upward in the long run for they may actually prove to be a handicap under new conditions, or in relation to other evolutionary developments.

"Take the evolution of wings by the birds for example: in spite of its immediate value and its brilliant promise it was a limited advance, for looking backward we can see that the birds have sacrificed their forelimbs to a restricted purpose and thereby cut themselves off from the tremendous power that these members might otherwise have acquired. To soar through the air appears to be full of poetic promise, but from the point of view of man with his two marvellous creative hands, a bird's life is only a little better than that of a lungfish. Wings are, from that point of view, a blind alley and it does not seem possible that the birds can ever escape from it to a better way of living. Some day they may go under like the lungfish because they chose the wrong road.

"The course of evolution is full of monstrous and absurd beasts so erratically fashioned that they proved to be their own undoing. Animals have repeatedly gone off in the direction of specializing some part of themselves until they have reduced the thing to futile absurdity. Some of the dinosaurs got bigger and bigger until their size became an outright handicap; the elephant, the hippopotamus, the gorilla are going the same way. The tusks, the horns, the teeth, the jaws on many animals have become so specialized that they bind these animals down to living a very limited kind of life.

Many adaptations start out by being useful but end up through excessive development in being a disadvantage. It is so common to find excessive specialization just preceding the extermination of a race that one comes to associate them together, and to accept the one as a sign of senescence presaging the other. The highly specialized animal is reaching the end of its blind alley.

"Then, too, the new inventions of one day may be carelessly thrown away in the next: the lung that was so precious to the Devonian fishes is not needed in the stable waters of today and so most fishes have discarded it entirely, or converted it into an air-tight swim-bladder. But should the world become arid again, these fishes, at least on the continents, would find themselves back where they were in the Devonian, suffocating in the mud and unable to save themselves. The legs that first purchased freedom on the land have been discarded by many animals because, just now, they can get along without them. The whales have gone back into an aquatic prison and undone the work of two hundred million years; now they are no better off, except for being warm-blooded, than the average fish so far behind them on the evolutionary road. Animals have thrown away their eyes, their teeth, their bones, their power of movement, even their power to live a free and independent life! The whole gamut of parasites, drawn from almost every branch of the vegetable and animal kingdoms, is a story of this degeneration.

"No, evolution is not all upward. It is only life flowing on through new forms, trying new ways of living, experimenting on an inconceivably varied scale. And for no purpose and with no meaning except that it wants to go on living. As we look back through the ages we can see that the circle of organic freedom has widened here or narrowed there as one branch or another has enjoyed new freedom in its separate time and place; but the upward phases are but infrequent, marked eruptions above the common level of flux and change. A line connecting them would zigzag along first one branch and then another. There is no sustained movement toward a special end, only an occasional carrying-over by some minor branch of the gains of one era to the potential victors of the next. It is this occasional and essentially haphazard carrying-over that has led to the increased freedom of the higher animals—the fishes, the amphibians, the reptiles, the birds, the mammals—and not a maintained, progressive movement. The only purpose of evolution is that life shall go on living in spite of all the obstacles that tend to put it down.

"Right there is its cardinal, most important feature: the stream of life tends always to persist, to carry on;

except that now and then, by the accident of mutation, it changes its course for some new way of living. It gets around obstacles by diversifying itself. It is out of the fact that it has changed its way of living so many times—and met so many obstacles—that it has come to be so diversified, that some branches of the stream have come into such great freedom, and that other branches have come only into blind alleys. But if it could speak it could truthfully say, 'I am what the obstacles that I have met have made me.' "

The Padre made a vehement gesture of denial.

"Oh, Joel, you are so right! . . . And so wrong! 'I am what the obstacles that I have met have made me—' Yes! But just accidental mutations— No! After all, the lungfish did achieve a victory over Devonian aridity even if he didn't solve all his problems. You can't dismiss that fact so lightly. I want to know, Why?"

"Why?" Joel shrugged his shoulders. "They used to say that the Why of life was one thing, and the How was another. Actually they are one and the same thing—just How. . . . The quickened moments of evolution have almost always coincided with the great upheavals of the earth's crust that have caused the climate of the earth to oscillate between extremes of heat and cold, of aridity and humidity. It has been these oscillations that have moulded the swift-swimming fish, the air-breathing amphibian, the desert-living reptile, the warm-blooded bird and mammal. The story of the Why-How of life is the story of the continuing conflict between its impetus to go on living and the ever-changing, infinitely complex environment in which it has to survive. The lungfish is—was—one of the battle-fields.

"We don't yet know how life comes to change its way of living. Mutation is at the heart of it, and mutation appears to be pretty much random variation in whatever characters you have to start with. But however it comes about, natural selection, as Darwin called it—or survival of the fittest, in Spencer's terms—trims most of the variants out and allows a few of them to go on: the final animal, be it bird or beast or worm is incidental—merely one of the many products which have been carved from the mutable organic stream. And in any case blind alleys are inevitable."

The Padre studied the floor between his feet for several minutes. When he looked up his face was wrinkled by perplexed interrogation.

"You believe that man is nothing more than one of the incidental products of this stream of life?"

"Certainly," Joel answered. "There is no evidence that evolution was intended solely to produce him. He is but one of its many products, not so much higher or lower than the rest, as just—more free. Nor is he the last—

the stream of life has long since flowed on past him. He is neither so recent a product as the horse nor so highly specialized, in respect to the general characters of the common mammalian stem, as the sea-cow."

The Padre interrupted:

"But just a minute—when you come to man you must admit that there is something that resides in him, and in him alone, that sets him apart from all the rest of the animal world. Something unique, more valuable, more precious. I grant you the evolution of man's mortal frame, but you must grant me that he is set apart from this stream of life that has produced him by something else, by some quality that savours of Divinity, a spark put into him along the road from beast to man. I don't know how I know it, Joel, but I know it's there! When I look at the infinite stars, at the infinitesimal atoms, when I look back over the course of your stream of life, then I am surest of myself. It is my special Inspiration. It makes me lift up my head in joy, in faith!"

Joel pondered over the Padre's remark. The force, the very tone of his voice carried his meaning better than his words. He was revealing himself now, disclosing the faith that was in him; a faith in a Spirit that transcended the mortal frame. He was not going to give it up easily, if at all, for to forfeit it was to let himself down into a pit of darkness in which there was no hope, only the chaos of a foul creation, the emptiness of a mortal flesh, both destined to become putrid with decay. His faith was in a Spirit that illumined the world and man with meaning, with an ultimate value and with a personal significance. His faith was in a Spirit that transcended all experience, all reality to have its being in some Perfection for which the finite world was but a means to a greater end, a vessel to hold for a short day an infinitely more precious content. That faith had been bred into him and nurtured into strength and still more strength. Was it so strong that it must swing an entire universe around his head and bring it into some special orientation with himself that was contrary to all fact? If so, the internal luminescence of it would blind him to its artificial nature; if not, then the truth would surely find its weakness out.

He did not like to be called a beast, Joel saw. . . . Was man a beast? In effect, the Church had long ago said yes—and no. Cursed by Original Sin, born in corruption, how could he be saved except by Redemption? The doctrine of Infant Damnation and the hope of Salvation were the answers which the Holy Fathers had sent back. In the old Jewish legend man was fallen from Grace; then a Saviour held down a hand to the grave to lift him back to his High Estate. . . .

It was man's cry against the terrifying world about

him, against the awfulness of nature, against the futility of life.

"No, Padre, we are only beasts. . . . It's strange how we consider ourselves the centre of the universe. The old boys used to think that the sun went around the earth, that the stars went around the earth, that everything went around the earth. They had difficulties making their geocentric system jibe with the observed movements of the heavenly bodies, so they got around their difficulties by compounding these movements out of cycles and epicycles and epi-epicycles. Copernicus showed them how simple it was, but when he took his figures to them they talked some metaphysical nonsense about the Perfect Nature of a Circle! Galileo made a telescope and found some irregularities on the Moon which he said were mountains, and some satellites around Jupiter which he said confirmed the Copernican theory; but he was damned for a heretic because everybody knew that the Moon must be a Perfect Body, and the Copernican doctrine had already been pronounced contrary to the Best Belief.

"Copernicus and Galileo and Newton did finally get us out of that metaphysical morass; but, you know, they didn't do much for us in a spiritual way. We still think that we are the centre of the universe; we still cling to a life-centred and a man-centred philosophy that is as artificial as the geocentric astronomy of the Middle Ages. We look upon the peculiar fact that the earth is placed a bit off-centre among the stars as due, perhaps, to some fanciful whim of the Creator.

"When we look about us we say, 'What a magnificent universe this is we live in! Aren't we important?' Every time a new star is discovered or a few million miles are added to the stellar spaces we expand accordingly. We see the universe around us as a frame for ourselves, and the bigger the frame the bigger the picture!

"It is man's colossal conceit! And when he sees that it does not jibe with the cold, hard facts of life and the universe around him, he rationalizes himself out of his insuperable difficulties by talking about the Redemption of the Spirit. . . .

"We are beasts, right along with the other flesh-and-blood beasts, one branch of the stream of life. We have not all the pages of the record, but we have enough of it to read the story: an unbroken stream from beast to man, life flowing on from one beast to another, changing its ways of living, getting around obstacles, first beast, then less beast, then more man. A beast more erect, with a larger cranium, less hair, shorter appendix, higher nose-bridge, higher forehead, sharper wits. There is the difference that sets him farthest apart from the other animals—his brain. There is his own unique and priceless specialty, a mass of nerve cells developed beyond any parallel in the animal kingdom! He has gone in for specializing that particular organ in preference to teeth or skin or bones. But the difference which it makes is not fundamental—it is only one of degree. . . .

"One wonders what terrific environmental pressure or what happy accident started that brain of his on its race to leave every other brain behind. There is no doubt that his hands played a large part in it. If there is anything divine in man, it is that his front paws were liberated at some remote time to the freedom which lets them clutch, carry, feel, measure, compare! Or it is the happy accident that drove him to use them in that manner. Perhaps he was driven by some emergency, some crowding danger that threatened his existence to use first one and then both paws, trying, shaping, making, doing, feeling; and his paws became hands and his brain was forced to grow to care for this vast wealth of sensory and motor experience; and as his brain grew his hands were there to serve it, whereupon they brought it new knowledge . . . and so the cycle sped on, faster and faster, until his brain grew into the colossal, complex organ which it is. All his art, his science, his philosophy, all his variegated activity must go back to these—" Joel held out his hands before him and wiggled his fingers in slow rhythms—"and to the fortunate combination of circumstances that permitted him, or forced him, through manual experience and manual experiment, to develop his wits.

"One imagines that perhaps he lived in a forest extending far north into the plateaux of Asia, a semitropical forest with a steady climate the year around. He walked more or less upright with the aid of his hands and lived by picking berries or fruits from the bushes or trees. He had a family life of sorts, keeping his young with him so that they had an opportunity to learn by example some of the cunning acquired by their elders. But Nature began to drive—the air grew colder and food grew scarcer and he was forced to leave his familiar forests and to migrate into open grasslands where he had to walk unaided by his hands. Perhaps there were no fruits or berries or sheltering trees and he had to tear up the grasses and grub among their roots for food, and to pile the stems about him to keep off the wind at night. Travel has a broadening influence: when he got hungry and his berries and fruits were gone he learned to catch the little field-mice that hid among the roots. He learned to kill the field-mice with a stick as they scurried out beneath his fumbling paws. He learned how to throw stones at them and how to match his wits against their cunning. Field-mice are fleet creatures and it takes quickness and dexterity to catch them. But our man had the advantage of standing on his hind legs, and of being able to pick up a stick or a stone in his fore-paws. And there was always the family; his children were by him and they had the invaluable opportunity to learn in a few days what he had found out by months or years of experience.

"Oh, that's just a picture! We don't know yet just how it happened, but some day we will. Our vision is obscured by distance, but it is penetrating that mist as Galileo's did when he first saw the mountains on the Moon through his hand-made telescope.

"But we can be sure that it is by these hands and the brain above them that man has come into his vast freedom. He has literally taken the world with them, both because he had them to use and because he had to use them. . . .

"But is the cycle of brains and hands coming to an end? Animals appear to evolve so far and then to stop. Man has changed very little in the past twenty thousand years, except in some minor details of hair and teeth. After the marked physical changes that transformed him from his pre-human ancestors, his bodily evolution appears to have slowed down, or to have stopped completely. It is doubtful if his intellectual evolution has not stopped in the same way. Of course, he has been accumulating, year after year, a greater store of knowledge which has given him a greater command of nature and himself. But is this enough? The accumulation of knowledge is a different thing from the capacity to use it, and there are many who claim that, in this respect, modern man is already a degenerate creature. One has only to look at his mental inertia, his destructive wars, his economic instability, his innate prejudice, his blind subservience to religion, his stupid politics, his dead resistance to changing his way of living, to wonder if he has reached his own blind alley. . . . Someone has cynically said that one of the marvels of Nature is the resistance which the human brain offers to the introduction of knowledge. One wonders that it got as· far as it did. For it works by repetitional rutting, and it sticks to its ruts until it is forcibly ejected. Its first concern is always with itself, and its greatest achievement is the profuse invention of labour-saving devices. Its highest aspiration is a Heaven where there are no clothes to put on and no exercise more strenuous than playing a harp! It is, like every other manifestation of life, intrinsically conservative: it travels in a straight line until it is forcibly deflected from its course. It appears to be headed for the same fate that overtook the dinosaurs, too specialized in one direction and too rigid in form and function to meet the dangers of another day.

"At the moment we have the run of things because

Cool

demarcated.

our hands and our wits can work for us. But let some new set of environmental conditions arise: let there come some new and devastating plague, or let the earth grow cold or hot or humid—all within the range of reason—and would our hands and wits suffice us? Perhaps . . .

"Oh, yes, by our standards we are very superior creatures! But it is probable that the mighty dinosaurs who lorded it over the Jurassic forests felt the same way as they uprooted the cycads and equisetums and trampled upon the little timid mammals that scurried among their roots. Someone has suggested that the dinosaurs were exterminated because these little mammals ate up all the dinosaur eggs! In any case, the dinosaurs are gone and a biped descendant of the creatures they despised now reigns. . . .

"It is very difficult to see ahead: I boast about these hands of ours, but how can I know that in gaining them we have not cut ourselves off from some powerful sense that is not yet evolved, a sense that could penetrate the mysteries of Nature that perplex us and lift us right out of this world and into another as lungs lifted the Devonian fishes on to the land? A sense that, perhaps, is even now being evolved from the rudimentary forelimbs of some primitive mammal in an obscure corner of Africa? Absurd? . . . The birds cut themselves off from hands by taking wings. . . . Man has been a rational creature for only a few thousand years, while the flow of life by evolution must be measured in hundreds of millions! Life may be breaking out through some obscure stream right now into a superior kind of animal, a superior way of living, and we would never know it!

"No, Padre. By the standards of the vast river of life that has produced us we are but a super-intelligent mammal momentarily over-running the globe and setting all manner of things upon it into whirling, confusing motions; creating our own criteria of superiority, creating our own far-off Divine Events, our own Divinities—to serve our ends."

VI

THE Padre rose and leaned upon the bulwarks, silent as though contemplating the beauty of the night. His back was turned toward Joel, who noted again his excellent physique. His broad flat shoulders were like those of some idealized sculpture and the profile of his half-turned head might have been a marble statue seen in the faint starlight. Joel thought about him as a specimen of the tall, broad-shouldered, long-headed type that had been bred within recent times out of the Anglo-Saxon stock. He seemed wrapped up in his own thoughts, so Joel kept silent, too. He wondered if he had offended him; he certainly had not meant to. There were certain facts from which all reasoning, all belief, must start. The essential thing was to have all the facts in hand, then each man could take his own interpretation. The Padre was not the kind of man to shudder at these facts, or to be easily shaken from his self-appointed course.

Joel got up and noted that the ship was again moving along the narrow Canal which stretched away into the darkness like a black ribbon. Occasionally they passed a dredge tied up for the night, or a few trees near a fresh-water well, but mostly there was only desert and that black ribbon stretching away, illuminated ahead by the searchlight fixed upon the bow.

Once they passed close to one of the signal stations whose duty it is to marshal into orderly procession the ships that pass from sea to sea. This one was a small white house set so close to the water's edge that it came into the glare of the bow-light. One could look down upon its red-tiled roof from the towering ship. A few date-palms and a small patch of grass around it afforded relief from the monotony of sand. A light, which from afar Joel had mistaken for a star, was swinging from a pole rigged like a ship's mast and set close to the water. Joel wondered what determined the right of way, for, when two ships passed, one had to tie up to the shore. He had heard that warships took precedence over every-thing else, and then ships bearing petrol or explosives. The latter were obviously a danger to the Canal, but it was very annoying to be on a supposedly fast mail-liner and to be shouldered aside by every oil-tramp that came along. The passage through the Canal took long enough, for that matter—from twelve hours upward according to the amount of traffic. No ship was allowed to proceed faster than six miles an hour. They had to

proceed with "extreme caution," and, moreover, the
wash at any greater speed would raise havoc with the
sandy shore. The infernal sand was always caving in,
and on either side there was a never-ending stream coming out of Arabia or Africa to keep up the supply. Two
billowing seas of sandy desert. Here and there was a
close-set picket fence, running parallel with the Canal,
which had been set up to keep the sand back.

You were always either fighting inanimate Nature,
Joel thought, or you were fighting other kinds of life.
Fighting not because you wanted to, but because you had
to, to keep alive! Life fighting for life against the wind,
the sand, the water, against every other living thing.
That was the only purpose that one could find in any
living thing—that was the first law of animate Nature—
life fighting for life. . . .

Joel tried to reconstruct a scene against the darkness
of the night: there is a big tree too large to encircle with
your arms, a smooth, grey-green tree that runs up four
or five times your height before it disappears into a dense
roof of leaves. At its base it has great sloping buttresses
that hold it upright in the soft soil; they remind you of
the ribs left in a bank of earth worn down by rain-water.
You can stand in the angle between two buttresses which
come up to your shoulder, and lean with your back
against the tree between them. When you close your

hand over their rounded edges they are like the arms of a great chair. The bark is cool and hard and covered with crisp grey lichens which scrape off beneath your fingers. Those buttresses—their slope, their rounded edges, their thickness between your fingers, suggest some living thing frozen into temporary immobility.

Leaning back against the tree you can look up at the green roof above you. It is a dense mat of branches and leaves intricately tangled and interwoven, so dense that the light just filters through it. That is why it is so dark around you. But when you look closer you see that those leaves are not the leaves of your tree but the leaves of plants that are growing upon its branches, countless creeping, climbing plants that hang down in a twisted, tangled canopy, plants that have climbed up and up to get the light. Behind your back is the stalk of one of them, a stalk nearly as big as your wrist that twists upon itself like a corkscrew as it runs up the trunk to disappear into the tangle of leaves. The stalk does not appear to be fastened to the trunk but you cannot budge it, you cannot pull it away far enough to slip your fingers under it. Beside it is another creeper-stalk, a small brown stem that zigzags back and forth in sharp angles up the trunk; at every zigzag it puts out a filament which ends in a little brown pad. When you tear the stalk away the filaments break off, leaving the pads adhering to the bark.

You cannot see the branches of your tree at all, so dense are the plants hanging from them. Some of them, born of a seed lodged in a crack and wanting soil, drop their aerial roots down to the ground where they dig themselves into the earth. The roots twist and turn as they come down and wind themselves around everything they touch, like snakes; and they dig themselves into the earth so far that you cannot pull them out, no matter how hard you try.

But some of the plants over your head seem to be growing out of the trunk of the tree itself. High up, there is a green fern which has a mass of brown roots adhering to the bark, and which spreads out its big fronds into a fan that is wider than a man's reach. The fronds have an intricate lace-like pattern that is everywhere the same except at the tips where a fuzzy grey bud is uncurling itself in an opening spiral. They seem to go on uncurling and uncurling—there is not one frond that is not uncurling at the tip. The pale-green fern is lovely against the dark-green leaves above it. Next to it on a dead branch is a gigantic plant—a mass of stems and leaves that must weigh five hundred pounds. It is an orchid from which there drops through the shadows a shower of pale-pink flowers, hundreds and hundreds of them, strung alternately along a slender stem with pale-green, heart-shaped leaves. It is a marvel that so large a plant can hang on to the smooth, hard bark. Back in a recess there is another flower, a white waxy blossom with a golden centre; as your eyes take in its shadowy features you discover a big dragonfly whose almost invisible wings are faintly outlined against a curving petal. The white blossom is growing upon a swinging root that is itself hanging from your tree. . . . One thing growing upon another, hanging on. . . . There is no wind and everything is perfectly still . . . and everything is silent; there is not a sound except your own heart beating in your ears.

Right beside your face there is a flat green rope which hangs down from above; its edges are armed with spikes as long as your finger and sharpened on both sides, sharpened like a razor. If you were to move your head against it, it would cut a deep gash in your cheek. All around you there are swinging stems armed with sharp thorns. Even the leaves on the bushes have saw-tooth edges—everything is armed! You are surrounded by a wall of trees, giant ferns, and bushes that are bound into a solid mass by creepers that climb in and out, and everything has a cruel, cutting edge. You are imprisoned by a vicious vegetation through which no soft-skinned

animal could make its way . . . and you are standing
in water, for the moss beneath your feet has let you down
until the green, scummy liquid has crept up around your
ankles. Treacherous green moss is everywhere and there
is not a dry place to which you can move—unless you
pull yourself up against the buttresses of your tree and
hang on. . . . It is hot, insufferably hot; so hot that the
sweat runs down your face and the stifling air makes you
sick and faint.

There is a sound in the dense bushes—they rustle as
they are pushed aside and the twigs lying on the ground
snap as they are crushed underfoot by some heavy animal. A small blunt head is thrust upward into an open
space—it has round, shiny eyes and black holes where
there should be ears—but it is lowered again quickly
as the animal comes on toward the clearing. Behind the
head is an incredibly long neck and a massive body from
which the tail tapers off and runs back thirty or forty
feet where it drags upon the ground. . . . You have
seen that animal before, somewhere. . . . It comes on
through the bushes with a slow, lumbering step, and
with its head held low so as to dodge the branches; and
every few steps it raises its head in a quick darting
movement to look about it. Once it opens its mouth
slightly and you see a red, sharply pointed tongue move
up and down between its lips. When the beast reaches

the clearing around your tree it straightens up and the head and neck tower to twice the height of your body. It takes a quick look to either side and, after a moment of immobility, it begins to nibble at the leaves around your head. Suddenly it shifts its weight and turns side-wise in its ardour to reach some tender shoot, and as the massive tail moves around through a half-circle the bushes and small trees are bent over and crushed as though they were fragile flowers. The beast rises slightly on its hind legs, throwing its tremendous weight on to its thick tail, and rests its forelimbs lightly against a nearby buttress. The legs are short and stumpy and sheathed in loose folds of skin and the toes are armed with sharp claws. You can see now that the skin is covered with scales which make a faint design of dia-monds, like the skin of a snake, and as the big neck moves from side to side the diamonds become stretched and twisted and the scales make a faint sound like the rustle of dry paper. You lay your hand upon the shoulder nearest you and it is cold . . . very cold. . . .

The Padre's voice suddenly broke in upon Joel's reverie.

"But that would be a denial of all our spiritual values, if we are only beasts, only better than the rest by a modicum of intelligence."

Joel's eyes lingered for a moment on the undulating

sand-hills: no, that was an anachronism, he thought, for that beast had been extinct a long time before those flower-bearing plants had been evolved. He looked around. The Padre was still leaning on the bulwark, his back turned toward Joel, and he turned his head slightly as he went on speaking.

"Look here—when the cave-man first drew a crude picture of a mammoth upon the wall of his cave he was giving expression to some impulse, some emergent or ascendant force that was more than the simple sum of his experience. He was at that moment different from his ancestors—something had been born, put into him!

"It is the same with his concept of Divinity, his striving for some ideal far above himself. This concept of Divinity has hovered about him, run through the fabric of his life, ever since we have had a record of his thoughts. I admit that it is variously coloured by his local time and nature, but it is always there, and its persistence must have some significance.

"You must admit that it is from his spiritual sense that man has gotten the best that is in him. Through it there has come to him his moral consciousness, his spiritual values—man's special blessing. Through it there has been revealed to him a special knowledge: there is nothing bestial about the Golden Rule!

"I'll take your science as a record of the flesh, but you

cannot take away from me my inner being, my bit of personal inspiration, that turns itself toward a spiritual standard that is far above me—like a magnet toward an unseen Pole." The Padre turned abruptly. "In that I am a man and not a beast!"

Several moments passed before Joel made any answer. Then he shook his head: "Your cave-man," he said, "is the key to the whole question. Without him we would be lost, but with him we can find our way. You have to understand that brain of his."

Joel had taken a metal key-ring out of his pocket and he was turning it between his fingers in an absent-minded way. His eyes rested on this trinket as he went on speaking:

"His brain worked in a quite simple fashion. On one side, so to speak, there was a storehouse where he could keep the sensory pictures—sights, smells, sounds, touch—of the world about him, and on the other side there was a delivery room where he could send out orders to his muscles for action; in the middle there was a clearing-house where he could sort everything out and size it up. All his life this brain of his was busy collecting sensory information in the one side, correlating that information in the central clearing-house, and acting upon the final product in the other. When he saw a mango, he ate it; when he saw a stick, he passed it by; but when he saw a mammoth, he ran!

"For there was another part to his brain, a fourth part which we can call his emotional sounding-board. It was just as important as the other three. Whenever any sensory picture came to his brain it passed, on its way to the clearing-house, across this sounding-board where it evoked some typical emotional reaction that was itself delivered to the clearing-house simultaneously with the original sensory picture. Thus the final sensory image consisted of a picture of the object coloured by the man's emotional reaction to that object. The mango evoked in him a sensation of delight mingled, perhaps, with hunger and desire; the stick produced no emotional response, while the mammoth filled him with awe and fear. He did not see hunger pains in the mango or awe and fear in the mammoth—these sensations were born entirely within him by resonance from his emotional sounding-board at the base of his brain. Yet, to him, they were just as real and just as much a part of the picture as the colour and smell of the mango or the length of the mammoth's tusks.

"That sounding-board was a very old part of his brain. The general pattern of it had been laid down back in bygone ages, and the typical emotional responses were much the same in all men, and relatively invariable. But the specific connexions between the sounding-board and the sensory paths to his brain were mostly left unattached, and remained free in each man to be plugged in with the sensory pictures from the world about him according to his individual experience. As his experience widened, more and more objects came to evoke some typical emotional response, and he came to classify the world more or less in terms of his emotional reactions: good things and bad things, pleasant and unpleasant, beautiful and ugly, indifferent and awful.

"That sounding-board played a very important part in his life. It served to reinforce the cold sensory image, to make it more vivid and to give it some personal colour; to give outside things a purpose, a meaning in his eyes. To meet his need it put delight in the mango; to meet his danger it put awe in the mammoth. It made the world significant—for himself.

"On the other hand it did things for him which thinking could not do. It was capable of calling forth in moments of anger or fright reserves of energy from his heart and tired muscles that his brain could never command. In emergencies when life was threatened it took charge of his brain even against his will and sent his body into quick action which he himself could not afterward understand. In a primitive way its pattern was laid down in such a manner as to safeguard him individually, and to safeguard the race, from annihilation. Secondarily, it was the driving force that motivated almost every move and directed his conduct almost every hour. It was the real spirit of his life.

"It sent him out to find a mate, dark or fair, brown eyes or blue. It set him to catching animals that he might clothe and feed her, and to guarding her from the dangers that beset them both. It built up his family, his tribal life, his inter-tribal warfare. It set him to watching the world around him with curious eyes, and to feeling, wondering, thinking. . . .

"Such was the nature of your cave-man's brain when he first saw a mammoth.

"Probably his experience with these creatures was such that when he saw one of them he was filled with fear: his breath stopped, his heart beat faster and thumped against his chest, his pulse throbbed in his temples, his knees shook under him, his mouth went dry, and he broke out in a cold sweat. But as soon as he recovered he ran back to his cave where he began to think about the awful creature, trying to fit it into its proper place in his life. . . . Little by little it slipped into the background of his thoughts, but he never really forgot it because its image seemed to lurk in the shadows and to hide around corners, and the memory of it, and of his fear, guided his footsteps through the dark jungles and coloured his fireside tales.

"Then there came a day when, while scratching around with a sharp pointed rock, he accidentally put some lines together so that they looked like a mammoth. The trick filled him with excitement, so he tried it again and again until he had a presentable picture. Perhaps it took him five thousand years, or perhaps it only took him five minutes, but in either case he was merely extending the combinations within his brain as every child does when it learns to draw. When he transposed the imagery of his senses into a crude picture of the original he was only channeling his activity into a new form of behaviour—drawing instead of running. The one was more advanced, but it was no more inspired. And his emotional stimulus was behind both of them.

"Ultimately he began to draw other kinds of pictures. There were many mammoths in his life: birth, death, misfortune, hope and despair, thunder and lightning—things that played just as large a part as real mammoths had ever played, and about which he knew even less. He could not draw them upon the wall of his cave because they had no lineal character, but as his artistic ability improved he learned to draw abstract conceptions of them, interpretations, explanations. These imaginary pictures were rougher, cruder even, than his scratches on stone, because that sounding-board of his exaggerated or distorted everything; its incessant rumbling made it difficult for him to see things clearly or to think about them straight. When he thought about the world at all he had to interpret not only its own complex features but also the maze of joy, sorrow, fear, hope, despair, desire, anger, love, awe, through which he saw it. In order to think along the shortest distance in a straight line he had first to penetrate his own emotional confusion. He had to stop to think—he had to stop the rumble of that archaic sounding-board which had come down to him through the ages, in order to hear his own thoughts. The trouble was, he did not often do it. From the beginning he felt first, and thought afterwards. . . .

"Primitive man was born in a dark jungle of supernaturalism, and only little by little has he built himself a home in the more reliable fields of reality. I admit that he found some spiritual values, as you call them, while he was lost in that supernatural jungle, but I deny that they were the fruit of its vegetation. They were, like the jungle itself, the fruit of his own imagination.

"Possibly the greatest of these is his discovery of himself—of self-appraisal. But there is nothing of Inspiration or Revelation in it; it is merely a new mode of cerebration, like drawing the picture of the mammoth, or like arithmetic, logic, or relativity. Man's appreciation of the Golden Rule came by experience, contemplation, and discovery, just as did his appreciation of the laws of gravity. The one waited for a Jew to formulate it in words and the other waited for a Newton. The spiritual appreciation of Hillel transcended that of the men about him, as did the physical appreciation of Newton. There was behind each a vast accumulation of experience waiting for an interpreter. . . . And behind each there was the cave-man's emotional urge.

"When you lay claim to a personal inspiration that turns you toward a spiritual goal, it is not an inspiration at all, but an expiration from that emotional sounding-board of yours modulated by your nativity, your culture, your experience. When the passive and indifferent wind of living plays upon you, you are set into reverberation and give out a certain tune. There are many different kinds of men in the world, as many different kinds as there are mothers to bear them and experiences to make them, and in the same wind each gives out a different tune.

"For that old sounding-board of man's has not lost any of its vibrant quality with time; and it still furnishes him with most of his driving power to go through life.

He has learned, a little, how to put his will upon its chords, how to still its reverberations so that he can think; but, being what he is, he needs, he must have emotional exercise lest his spirit atrophy and fade away. Now that he no longer gets it from a cave-man's life he turns to other sources—to music, drama, literature, and art. He loves it—he loves to have that sounding-board struck into reverberation, to have it pounded upon until its music jingles in his ears and tingles in his toes— and it is well that he should if for no other reason than that through this exercise he will come into a better understanding of himself. As yet, however, he is still your cave-man, squatting on his haunches and bewitched by his picture on the wall. . . . The Sacred Soul of Man—the Devil that lives in the mammoth! He would have awakened to the absurdity of it long ago were it not for his emotional confusion; he still cannot see himself except through the raptures of his body! But perhaps as time goes on he will learn the nature of those raptures, and his vision of himself will clear.

"But he is old enough now to throw away his Inspiration, Revelation, Special Providence, and all the rest of his cave-man's pictures, and to put himself back into his proper place in Nature, back among the beasts, the birds, the flowers. He is old enough to see himself as he really is—a mammal among mammals, fighting the same fight as all the rest. He is old enough to know that in the years to come he may be crowded out like the prehistoric monsters of the past, while life breaks out in some ascendant form that is better fitted to survive. . . .

"If he wishes to know where life begins and ends, then he must study it, see how it works and what it is. Perhaps the perfect knowledge will not come to him until he has evolved some superhuman sense, some novel way of living; or perhaps it waits only for the discovery of some new mode of cerebration, like your picture-boy. Or it may never come to him, for the stream of life may shift to some other bed before that time, and leave him a blind alley."

VII

Joel tossed the key-ring with which he was playing into the air, and thrust it back into his pocket. He turned to the bulwark and leaned over to watch the series of smooth waves that marched alongside at the foot of the steep prow.

"What a pessimist you are, Joel! . . . Though I must say you do talk well for the first cousin of an anthropoid ape."

The Padre squirmed himself into a more comfortable position, half on his back.

"But you *are* discouraging. I still think there is some loophole in your damnable mechanistic doctrine through which I can escape. Life and evolution must have some meaning for me as well as for you, but as you interpret it, it is meaningless.

"Even if I grant that my emotional instincts are— what shall I say, animalistic reactions?—and therefore unworthy of an ultimate appeal I still am not satisfied on the grounds of pure reason with your explanation of things. Beyond the realm of the phenomena which we can see and measure, behind the whole process of evolution and within the warm pulse of life itself, there is an Unknown which neither you nor I nor any man can ever fully comprehend. You as a scientist have your attention fixed upon the known while I, being what my sounding-board has made me, prefer to turn my eyes toward that more distant horizon.

"I cannot remain content with a philosophy that is out of step with science; I want to go along with science and understand it. The scientific spirit is one aspect of life which has proved its worth, both pragmatically and intellectually—yes, and æsthetically, too. There is grandeur and beauty in your scientific saga as in the Psalms of David— I love them both. I am a man of two parts: a man of faith and a man of action. It is not enough for me to say, 'God made it thus'; for I must always ask myself, 'Do I see it as God made it?' So I would step closer and obtain a nearer vision of the Unseen by treading the path of reason, by walking along with you. . . .

"At night, after the African drum which does duty for a church bell has rolled out its summons to prayers, I ponder on it; when the village is safely asleep under the heavy-eyed and misty stars and there is no sound except the incessant whirring of cicadas or the occasional bark of a stray ape up to some mischief in the maize,

I walk among the acacias with evolution in one hand and astronomy in the other. I am lost, not in a web of emotional confusion, but in the sheer tangle of my reason trying to put them all together and to make them fit into a coherent whole. I go from a theory of Special Creation to one of Evolution without finding any that satisfies me, and without finding a God Who is compatible with either. . . . What you say about man is true, he is a beast; and life is filled each day, as throughout its evolution, with pitfalls, with blind alleys. The bitter cruelty of man, the hardness of his lot, his hapless fate, are difficult to reconcile with the smooth orbits of the stars, the geometry of a crystal. Life alone seems to be devoid of order. Only in us is God incomprehensible . . . but surely He has not so hidden His countenance that we cannot obtain some little light to guide our steps. . . . Only by seeing God in us are we comprehensible. I do not ask to know the ultimate beginning and the ultimate end of life, but only how to find the open road. . . . Which way, O Life, shall I turn now?"

"I cannot help you." Joel turned back from the water. "Isn't it said that you can only find God by faith alone? . . . Modern science cannot take you any nearer your unseen horizon than could the science of ancient Greece or Babylonia. Some scientists think that it can, but they are only fooling themselves. Scientific knowledge comprises the world of the known and the knowable, and hypotheses based upon the known are scientific hypotheses; the validity of science and its hypotheses rests upon proof by correspondence with reality. Beyond these there is only the great vacuity of the unknown, and science cannot stop you, and fundamentally is not interested, if you as a man of faith or as a philosopher wish to jump off into that vacuity; except to say that there is nothing in history to indicate that you will accomplish anything by doing so. . . . Special Creation is as good a doctrine to jump into as any other, for all those who would instil something into matter in order to make life are only Special Creationists squeezed out of shape by trying to square themselves with experience. Whenever they come to a tempting gap in our knowledge—whether it be vital spirits and animal heat or the limitations of physical measurement—they put their fingers on it and say: 'Here is God.' At heart, what they want to do is to put into the Universe *purpose* where there is only *process;* to put plan *before* the event rather than *after*. They want to mark the sparrow's fall, not by the laws of Chance, but by the Hand of God. So they peer out past the outlying ramparts of science to discover if there is a Deity hovering near; not realizing, when they find Him, that either He must devour them or they must devour Him—either they must post a sign toward science saying, 'Here is where you get off!' or they must be prepared to amputate a slice off their Deity at any future time and to graft it on to the body of verifiable knowledge. . . . No, you can never find God by walking with me. . . . When you start back for your temple in the jungle you should leave your biology at home. For life is a phenomenon of Nature and the more we dig into natural law the more we find of the laws of chance."

The Padre shook his head, and held up a hand as though to stop Joel from talking. After a moment he got up and rested his elbows on the opposite bulwark, staring into the darkness ahead.

"You cannot so lightly discount the Unknown, Joel. As a scientist you do not neglect the unknown. You calculate on it in every step you take. You extrapolate from the known to the unknown every day, and, if I understand correctly, that is in great part how you make progress. You do not speak of 'Jumping off into the unknown' when you speculate, as I presume you must, on matters pertaining to geology, or to your lungfish. You speculate in part because you want everything to be reasonable, to fit together, to make sense.

"Yet when you add it all together, in your total philosophy you dismiss the greatest unknowns of all—the

Beginning and the End of things, the Whence and Whither—with a shrug. Almost a contemptuous shrug. You speak of the laws of chance with respect, but you are almost resentful of what I call God. Are you afraid of Him? Is it such a small gap in your knowledge that you do not know why evolution has come about, why we and the sun, moon and stars are here, that you can ignore it as unworthy of your consideration?

"I suspect you are overlooking a great many Unknowns. You know a lot about that lungfish of yours, but come with me up the Ruvuma River and see something with which you are possibly not so familiar. See my boys clearing the jungle to set out plantains and maize in long, straight rows. See their wood-working shops where they make baskets and tables and chairs. Watch them in their homes, see how they love their children, see their courage against adversity, their fortitude against suffering. See how grateful they are not only for the quinine and little medicines we give them, and the occasional surgery, but for every new thing we bring them—for the schools where they can not only study their own dialects but learn Swahili and English, if they have a talent for it; for their increasing knowledge of themselves and of the outside world. Yes, and for the Golden Rule. Oh, they are bad, sometimes, very bad, but they can also be very good. Sometimes I am very angry with them, but mostly I love them, lowly creatures that they are. . . . Did the lungfish evolve new eyes when it crawled out upon the land? I do wish you could come up the Ruvuma River with me, Joel; you would enjoy my black boys."

"They aren't 'lowly creatures,' Padre. I don't like that expression. There is a wide range of individual aptitude in every race, but there is no convincing evidence that intrinsic aptitude differs significantly among the major races of mankind. Send them to college and they will be teaching biology and physics. And theology, I dare say. Only I wish they'd stick to biology and physics."

"You really think they are capable of going that far? I don't mean theology—" the Padre laughed, "—I mean just biology and physics?"

"Of course they are. It's largely a matter of background and training just as in any animal stock.

"Of course you love them, and they love you. . . . And I am not resentful of your God. Neither am I afraid of Him or of the Unknown, and neither do I dismiss the Unknown with a contemptuous shrug. Only as a scientist I am convinced that I do not know anything about God and I cannot talk about something that I know nothing about. He may be there, but I cannot accept as proof any of the evidences that have hitherto been presented, and, as the astronomer La Place told

Napoleon *à propos* of astronomy, one has no need of that hypothesis. As a scientist I do extrapolate into the unknown, yes, but only where I can test the extrapolation. One cannot test your hypothesis, and however well it may satisfy your hunger for an answer to the Great Unknowns, it does not satisfy mine. It is, in fact, no answer at all. It will not jibe with the lungfish, with any of the verifiable facts of this admittedly grotesque scheme of things. I would rather say that I don't know, and stick to what I do know. It is one thing to speculate about the Unknown—it is another to let it shape the pattern of your life in any way. The one is harmless, the other dangerous. You would still be in Tanganyika whatever kind of God you believed in, a good God, an evil God or one who was both good and evil, or no God at all."

The Padre laughed. "Yes, I think you are right. . . . And you can't prove the existence or non-existence of God by argument. It is a matter of faith—I choose to believe, and you do not."

"Just a moment." Joel interrupted. "I have not denied the existence of any one or an infinite number of deities. I simply choose not to talk about that about which I know absolutely nothing. You would, I take it, persuade me to take your God into my scheme of things. Now, I ask you, Is your God Good, or is He Evil, or is He both? We can start from there. . . ."

The Padre laughed again, roguishly. "No, Joel, we are not going to start from there. We are going to start from your lungfish. I think you contradict yourself! You say that life is a phenomenon of Nature; yet life has risen in spite of Nature, it has risen above her until it over-rides her, uses her, dominates her. You can't do that with a *part* of Nature without adding something to it. You talk about life flowing on through new forms, trying to keep alive. Almost waiting until accidental mutations come to its advantage, yes, but all the time there is this will to live. And yet you do not know what life is, this life that flows through bird and beast and man. The biologists, I think, talk about protoplasm as the 'physical basis of life,' which implies to me that protoplasm is the machinery by which something that I call 'life' carries on this business of living. Can your protoplasm explain the insurgence that has carried life over obstacle after obstacle in its evolution? Can it explain the sentience that every organism shows to some degree? Can it explain the fight that every organism puts up to keep on going?

"Perhaps we cannot see ourselves clearly because of our emotional confusion, but we should certainly be able to see an amoeba, let us say, without prejudice. Yet your protoplasm does not tell you why an amoeba grows, why it reproduces itself, why it is so nicely adjusted to its environment, or why it goes on being an amoeba instead of turning suddenly into something else. Life is different from the rest of Nature because it is forever pushing uphill in its search for freedom, while the universe is forever cooling off, running down."

"No, there is something wrong with your cave-man's picture. There is something missing from it; something that not only supplies the will to live but pushes forward, even when it gets itself into blind alleys! That is why I say that you don't know what life is—you only know *how* it lives, and there is a big difference."

Joel turned back to the yellow, fan-shaped beam that cut sharply through the surrounding blackness and illuminated the water and the sandy shore ahead. It seemed to possess some tangible golden substance which it sprayed like paint over the landscape, and as it crept forward at a steady pace the formless shadows which it engulfed became stones, or posts, or eerie masses of machinery that were sharply defined in scintillating radiance. He straightened up and ran his hands along the cold iron edge of the bulwark.

"No, we don't know what life is, but we must find out what it is from how it works. I admit, so far as protoplasm is concerned, that there may be something wrong with the picture. . . . I sometimes wonder if we don't look at life, at protoplasm, in the wrong way. I wonder if we do not see it backwards, upside down, wrong side out! Perhaps that slimy jelly is not really the 'physical basis of life,' as Huxley called it, but merely a pile of driftwood, a mantle of debris thrown up around the centre where life is. If so, perhaps it obscures the living centre from our view. We would have to tear the jelly away, as you tear away the slime from around a spitbug, to find the living focus at its heart."

The Padre squatted on the floor again and thrust his hands into his coat-pockets.

"Are you going over to a dualistic theory of mind and matter?" he asked, looking up at Joel with an amused smile.

"No," Joel answered, "nothing like that. I remain a mechanist. I am only going consistently back along the course of mechanistic evolution. We have asked ourselves, Did the reptile exist before the mammal, the invertebrate before the vertebrate, the protozoan before the metazoan; why not ask, Did not life exist before the mantle of flesh in which we now find it clothed? I was thinking that perhaps it did. I was thinking—if I may indulge in pure fantasy—that at the heart of that gelatinous blob of protoplasm there may be something ut-

terly primitive and simple—something, say, like a whirlpool."

"Heavens!" the Padre interjected. "Isn't protoplasm
complex enough without putting a whirlpool inside it?"

Joel shrugged his shoulders. "That's the trouble—it's
too complex. It has the complexity of a multitude of
effects that can issue from a single source. I was looking
for the source, something that is simplicity itself. That
is why I chose a whirlpool—a whirlpool of sunlight, if
you wish, or, if you prefer a more technical term, call
it an eddy in the Second Law of Thermodynamics."

The Padre laughed. "I'm worse off now than I was
before."

Joel flashed a smile at his companion, then jumped
down from the bracket and paced back and forth along
its edge.

"What I mean is"—he stopped suddenly to make a
gesture with his hand—"did you ever have among your
toys a gyroscope? Do you remember, when the wheel
was spinning rapidly, how the thing felt in your hand?
How it resisted you when you tried to turn it over,
pushing back against your fingers with such uncanny
power? And when it was forcibly laid on its side, how it
straightened itself up at once? Well, life is something
like that. . . .

"It's a crude analogy, but try to imagine a flowing

river and note where it strikes against a sandbar of just the right shape." Joel pointed his fingers at the Padre's feet and began to make rapid, circular motions. "Part of the water is deflected from its course and thrown into a whirling motion. That whirlpool is a dynamic entity, a thing apart from the smoothly flowing river in which it has its being."

He waved his hand toward the brilliant stars above them.

"Now turn from the river of water to the universe around us: you say the universe is running down. I would put it another way—I would say that we live in a river of free energy that tends to flow from a higher level to a lower one. The living organism is an arrangement of matter engaged in absorbing, storing, and spending a little of this energy. By doing so, it seems to swim against the major stream.

"Perhaps life is to this river of energy what the whirlpool is to the flowing water, a consequence of sunlight striking upon the dust and being deflected into some special motion, just as the whirlpool is a consequence of water striking upon the sandbar."

Several minutes passed before the Padre spoke. The silence was broken only by the notes of the ship's bell striking the hour, and the lower tones of the forecastle bell echoing back a few seconds later.

"But life has a purpose, it has power and knowledge--
there must be **something** to it besides a mere spin of
energy like a whirling dervish in the wind——"

"Right!" Joel interrupted him. "That is just why I
called it a whirlpool. . . . A whirlpool, you see, when
once set in motion tends always to continue in that motion, and it opposes destruction with an almost intelligent resistance. If friction wears the whirlpool down,
then the river speeds it up again so that it is always whirling, whirling. It has a will to live that is born of its
momentum. And it has power, borrowed from the
river, to resist invasion or deflection from its course. And
it has knowledge, for it tends always to right itself if it
is pushed out of a position of equilibrium.

"Life is like a whirlpool in many ways. . . . When
once set a-going it spins on and on. It is not self-
sustained because its energy is but borrowed from the
river, being constantly renewed upstream and dis-
charged below. If you deprive it of that energy it dies.
In its tendency to spin on for ever there is life's purpose—to go on living. So long as the sunlight flows, the
whirlpool is charged with power, for the energy which
is turned into it can reappear as force to resist invasion
or deflection from its course. But most importantly, the
whirlpool is intelligent for it is endowed by its dynamic
nature with discrimination toward the world about **it,**

and with the tendency to seek those states which disturb it least. When it is disturbed it automatically reacts to bring itself back into a balanced state, into a condition of well-being. It is that dynamic balance which is life's sentience; it is the prompt reaction, when that balance is upset, that is life's activity. To paraphrase an old law of physiology, 'life never acts; it only reacts. . . .'

"There are the cardinal features of life, born of the momentum of a whirlpool: a will to live, power to live, intelligence to live. There is no cell, there is no protoplasmic jelly, yet life is on its way. Before it is ever clothed in that jelly it wants to live and it has the power to live, and within limits it knows how to go about living. And all that it wants is to go on living!"

"Then what is the protoplasmic jelly for?"

"It is not *for* anything. It is a pile of debris around the whirlpool. . . . See how the leaves and twigs float into the whirlpool in the river and are picked up and hurled about until they are thrown out upon the shore: so molecules float into our whirlpool in the sunlight and are momentarily caught up in the vortex of its activity and get battered about until they are broken and rearranged into complex organic compounds before they are shot out at the periphery. Some of them stick together and form a jelly that is pushed out and out as far as the whirlpool can push. . . . Thus is your protoplasmic mantle spun and you have a cell—an extraordinarily complex mass which the organic chemist hasn't unravelled yet, and the physical chemist is jolly well lost in the intricacies of its enzymes and surface tensions; but who ever saw a junk pile that wasn't a bewildering conglomeration?

"Watch how it works. Our whirlpool is surrounded by an environment that bombards it continually and tends to choke it up with indigestible debris. It must do battle with that environment every second, matching only its momentum against whatever obstacles it meets. With good luck, the battle may be drawn out endlessly, while the whirlpool cries, 'Won't die!' and environment cries, *'Must die!'* . . . *'Won't die!—Must die!—Won't die!—Must die!'* . . . There is the pulse of life that beats in every cell—there is the pulse by which life has beat its way up the long road of evolution—and the first protoplasm was the first beat of that pulse, it was born of the first battle.

"I say with luck, for just as life came into being by the chance encounter of sunlight and matter, so its continued existence from hour to hour hangs on the chances that it can keep on going in the face of injury, that it won't be suffocated by its own cellular debris. The evolution of the first cell was an infinitely bigger jump than the evolution of ape to man. That cell is a dynamic mass of enzymes and reactive compounds so equilibrated with each other that, if pressed upon at any point, the impulse is transmitted inwardly and answering forces from within are carried back. If the mantle is bruised, fresh materials are forced into the hole and the wound heals.

"The protoplasmic mass is itself an encumbrance. By shutting out the sunlight it tends to pull the whirlpool down; as the pile of debris grows bigger the dynamic center spins more slowly, until it all but dies. . . . But in dying, it divides into two cells. Look at how a whirlpool dies—you can watch the process in your bathtub, or in a whirlwind or a waterspout. Viewed from the side, a symmetrical whirlpool looks like two cones meeting at their points. So long as it is going at full speed these cones adhere together, but as it slows down they pull apart so that there is only half a whirlpool above and half a whirlpool below, separated by a more or less inactive region in the middle. As the pile of debris around our whirlpool of sunlight increases in size, it is retarded until it breaks into two parts; in the centre the forces which push out the protoplasmic jelly are diminished, and this jelly, falling back through instability and disintegration, shrinks into the cell—and itself divides into two parts—into two equal daughter cells each having one-half a whirlpool. But in the matter of whirlpools a part is as good as a whole and, as soon as the retarding effect is removed, the missing halves restore themselves and begin to throw up new piles of protoplasmic jelly, continuing until they themselves, choked down again and dying, divide; thus one cell into two, two into four, four into eight, *ad infinitum*. So the whirlpool escapes from the pile of debris which accumulates around its edges by dividing and starting over.

"It is, by the laws of chance, impossible for a single whirlpool to last for ever because sooner or later some accident would inevitably destroy it. But by multiplication of its numbers its chances of survival are also multiplied; and so our would-be immortal whirlpool escapes the threat of death that lurks in the laws of chance even while it is escaping the threat of death that lurks in the accumulation of debris around it. . . .

"It has won three battles, it is three paces nearer to realizing its innermost wish for immortality. It has escaped the threat of death that lurks in its random encounters with environment; it has escaped the threat of death that lurks in the debris piled up as a result of these encounters, and it has escaped the threat of death that lurks in the very laws of chance by multiplying itself into a large number of individuals. It has become an organism that grows spontaneously to a fixed size and shape, and that heals itself after injury; it has a rudimentary perception of the world about it and tne necessary intelligence to interpret the information in relation to its own well-being; it has power to gain its ends, and power stored away in fuel for those hours when the river is not flowing; it undergoes spontaneous and perfect division when it reaches maturity, and thus tends to multiply itself in numbers and to spread into all the habitable parts of the earth. And it has a will to live that carries it on and on!

"We need not worry yet about the complexity of the sandbar upon which our whirlpool spins; for in these days our ideas of matter, like real sandbars, are shifting overnight. There are several different kinds of life—perhaps the green plants and the animals, the sulphur bacteria, the filterable viruses, and many other kinds of living things have each had a different origin, or perhaps they are only different habits of the same life-stream. But they are all just local eddies in the river of energy that flows around them. The apparent complexity of the higher animals tends to obscure life's real simplicity, for out of its long history it has acquired a manifold design. There have come to be cells which, though dividing, yet remain together in delicate balance to make a multicellular organism. These cells have come, through the potentialities of the mother cell, to be differentiated into a body of highly specialized parts—

skin, muscles, nerves, glands, receptors, bones—so that by this division of physiological labour the efficiency of each is increased; but these cells have no powers or properties that are not inherent in the fundamental plan.

"During this evolution into a body of specialized parts it has come to pass that certain cells have been set aside to carry on the stream of life—the germ cells— by beginning anew and spinning another body. Perhaps this is because the great specialization of the body cells renders them unfit to serve a genetic role, and perhaps there is an advantage to be gained by putting the germ cells away where they will not be bruised by a rude world. But it is thus that death finally came about. The lower animals that multiply by division are immortal for, as someone has said, you cannot speak of death where there is nothing left to bury. But the flesh of the higher animals is too specialized, this pile of debris is too cumbersome, to be of further use; so after it has matured and been given an opportunity to pass on the seed of life, it is thrown aside. And the whirlpool escapes through the germ cell, to fight another battle. . . .

"It has come about that organisms have learned to draw the energy to keep their whirlpools going not directly from the sunlight but from the dead substance of other organisms: until the fisherman lives upon fish which live upon crustaceans which live upon infusorians which live upon diatoms, while only the diatoms still live directly in the sunlight stream. Life has gained, perhaps, its greatest freedom by this cannibalistic habit, but it has not changed its nature, for, fisherman or diatom, it is still sunlight spinning within the cell.

"It has come about that the natural forces of that primordial organism are made manifest in ways that are variegated beyond belief;

"Until life lives in bodies that are big and small, in bodies that are born from a spore, from an egg, or from a mother's womb; in bodies that last a week, a month, or threescore years and ten; in bodies that are of two sexes or only one; in bodies that have long noses, short noses, or no noses at all;

"Until life has broken itself into hundreds of thousands of species and has spread itself into the depths of the ocean, the heights of the mountains, the air, into caverns, coal-mines, icebergs, hot springs;

"Until the scorpion has poison on the tip of its tail and the cobra poison at the roots of its fangs; until the flower has honey in its heart and the bee honey in its comb;

"Until the spider revels in the shadows and the bird in the sunshine and the biologist in all of them!

"Yes, life has spun itself into a web that is infinitely complex with interrelations, interdependencies—but it makes no difference; it is the same sunlight spinning the same matter in all of us—in you and me, the bird, the tree, the worm, the diatom; only the life-habit of the whirlpool, the number of whirlpools in our bodies, and the intricate pattern of their arrangement are in each of us a little different. . . .

"One should not be surprised that there is a remarkable 'fitness' between life and the world it lives in, for the fitness of the living organism to its environment and the fitness of environment to the living organism are as the fit between a die and its mould, between the whirlpool and the river bed. What we should note is that the fit is neither perfect nor permanent, because environment is not constant in its character for a fleeting instant; it changes with every breeze and sound, with every light and shadow. The battle is never finished and the pulse of life beats on . . . *Won't die!—Must die!— Won't die!—Must die!* . . . It throbs anew each second into the substance of its flesh, into its healing, its reproduction, its rhythms, its activities, its further evolution—into its innermost wish. . . . But still it is not intelligent enough to keep itself out of blind alleys—of mud or philosophy, or of speculating about its own nature!"

Joel laughed and shook his head. "No, I do not know what life is. But I think that it is something like that; like a whirlpool stirred up in the dust by sunlight that, spinning on and on, of its own momentum presses always against its environment where the blind alleys are cut off and the rest escapes through different ways of spinning."

"IT IS a beautiful idea!" The Padre looked up at Joel and smiled.

"Beautiful!" Joel stepped up on the bracket and glowered down at him. He folded his arms in an attitude of belligerent scorn. "Beautiful? How can you call it beautiful? Then you don't see it! Look at it again—see that whirlpool in the river that drowns the bodies of men. . . . See that whirlpool in the sunlight that vomits its refuse around its edge, pushing it farther and farther away until it can push no more! That flesh is but the excrement accumulated around the spinning vortex; the whole body of life, its tissue, its bone, its nerves are but waste products that would have been gotten rid of by the whirlpool if it could, and failing that have been disposed of in the way least offensive to its activity. The lovely features of that flesh have been moulded by being thrown haphazardly against the world! The *beautiful* temple of flesh, indeed!

"It is only choking refuse, aching for immortality with an ache that is naught but the shriek of a brake on a wheel! Its first birth was an escape from an accident, and its continued existence from hour to hour, from generation to generation, from race to race, is but a succession of escapes from a succession of new accidents— dodging the death to which it is doomed when the sun stops shining; and even if the sun shines for ever, life will stop first, for the doom of death was laid upon it at the moment of its birth—it lives only until the last momentum meets the last inertia—until the last accident! Is an accident *beautiful?*

"Its spinning heart lives by taking the easiest way, the one least likely to inconvenience it! The warmth of its body is but a result of friction! Its very sense and perception are but mere echoes of the fact that it wants to be let alone! The power—the glorious power of life!— is stolen out of its heart against its innermost wish, and is given up only that it may stop a further theft! Life's vitality, its activity, its whole evolution are but the remonstrance of that whirlpool against being disturbed from its eternal motion—its eternal, eternal momentum! Is momentum *beautiful?*

"I said that there is no goal to evolution except that life shall go on living, that there is no maintained direction except the one in which it is already moving. I should say that there is nothing but a long-drawn-out battle between matter and motion, and a battlefield strewn with debris. . . . Damn it all! Can you find anything in that picture to call it *beautiful?*"

"Yes," the Padre answered promptly, "I can . . . if one individual can see and hear and talk to another, and if they can make each other smile . . . then force has met force agreeably and to their mutual benefit— for life travels faster in co-operation than otherwise, doesn't it?"

He looked up, laughing. "There must be something wrong with your theory, Joel, because we start with two mutually repellent whirlpools that want to be let alone and in the end have them coming together to their mutual acceleration."

"Yes," Joel answered, laughing himself now. "But only because that is the mutually easiest way!

"I'm sorry," he went on; "I was afraid—I only wanted you to see life as it is for its own sake, and be prepared to take the consequences; and not for some anthropo-morphic idea of what is or is not beautiful."

"Why?"

"Because the idea that just because we find a thing pretty, it's good, or true, or has any significance what-ever beyond the eye of the beholder, has done immeas-urable harm. We must see the mammoth and not our fear or our delight in it."

The Padre looked up at Joel with a quizzical smile and suddenly broke into a loud laugh.

"I'm glad to know you were afraid," he said.

But Joel did not get the drift of his remark. He moved to stretch his cramped arms and legs and was surprised to see that the ship had come into Port Saïd and was moving slowly down the channel to an anchorage. He had no idea what time it was, but he guessed that it must be close to morning. So they were at Saïd at last! A feeling of intense relief mingled with revulsion swept over him. He loathed the sea—he'd never get into a ship again! Why on earth should anyone put himself into that prison except out of sheer necessity? After incarceration on a boat for two weeks you loathed everything connected with it; the mere gestures of civility became a painful bore; you knew every face, everything it had to say, every thought behind its eyes, every cravat its owner wore. Why, on God's earth, did that Frenchman pick out a pink one with yellow fleurs-de-lis if it was to be the only one he had? And why did they choose to paint the dining-saloon with red parrots and purple monkeys when you had to look at them three times a day for fourteen days? Who invented the damnable deck-chairs that broke your back and cut your legs off above the knees and why do French colonials have twelve children? And why is one of them always cross-eyed?

Joel shrugged his shoulders. There seemed to be no passageway through the maze of dark forms that rode at anchor in the coaling-basins and along the channel. Their masts and spars and lines made an intricate web of black against the faintly luminous sky. There were big ships and little ships, some with their deck-lights burning and some shrouded in darkness except for the riding-lights fixed upon the mast-stays. Joel could make out the names of a few of them as the light from the *Dumbea* passed across their overhanging sterns or their pointed bows— *Razmak:* now by her marks she was a P. and O. boat, and she'd be coming in from India; *Hakosaki Maru:* she'd be from the land of cherry blossoms and temples lacquered in blue and red and gold; she'd have called at Shanghai, near the mouth of the Yangtse in the valley of which lives one-tenth of the world's population, and again at the old pirates' harbour of Hong Kong where the mountains of China drop abruptly into the sea; *Llanstephan Castle:* she'd be going down the East Coast to South Africa and she'd call at Mombasa, Zanzibar, and Dar-es-Salaam; *Finisterre:* now she'd be a bug-ridden tramp knocking about

Heaven knows where or what for—she didn't look as if she could ride out a heavy sea!

New ships and old ships, made fast stem and stern to buoys anchored in parallel lines along the Canal. Ships asleep, and soiled as all ships soil when they come into port, to lie passive and unresisting while coolies swarm over them like ants to steal away their cargo or dump baskets of filthy coal into their hatches. But ships sleeping lightly, apt to wake up at any moment and with a long blast on the whistle shove off to sea. Tomorrow they would be riding along the blue horizon with their decks scoured down to clean white wood and their brass newly gleaming in the morning sun, proudly throwing off a crested wave on either side. But now they lay sleeping quietly, dark hulks against the sky, while lighters and small craft crowded into their darker shadows like flotsam lodged against a rock. Silent ships, asleep; there was some magic locked up in their sombre masses that, if released, would spring forth with life and meaning. . . .

Above the masts and funnels great lamps covered by conical reflectors threw light upon the coaling-basins and the sides of the Canal. Behind them only gloomy, cubical shadows marked the streets where they ran back into the Arab quarter. The scene, with its suggestion of mechanism here and there, was strangely like a modernistic stage-setting. A plume of steam escaping from a nearby vessel waved slowly from side to side as the breeze played with it. It was illuminated from above into faintly phosphorescent rings and spirals that vanished into thin air.

Once a searchlight shoved its ghostly finger through the night and moved it with incredible speed here and there in crazy paths, lighting up for brief instants bits of ship's gear, spidery coaling-towers, giant derricks; it rested for a moment on the grey-clad figure of a sailor stretched face upward on a deck; the man rolled over and the luminous finger shot downwards to the black water, revealing a boat being poled by an Arab in a banded gown; then it moved across more black water to come to rest pointing down along a ship's ladder into a dory waiting for its passenger. The passenger turned out to be a portly man in baggy white clothes, with a briefcase under his arm and a red fez on his head. He chose to descend the ladder backwards and he stopped every few steps to look up and gesticulate an emphatic farewell to some invisible person above him. He had hardly reached the dory when the searchlight was abruptly switched off.

Almost as if this were a signal, a gramophone on the deck which he had left began to play a dance tune.

Joel stiffened slightly with attention: the tune had merry notes that were syncopated into delicate crescendos; it seemed to spin a web of sound upon the still night air. It caught his pulse and breathing in its measures and forced them into its own rhythm with a sharp sense of pain. He shut his eyes and gave himself up to the enchantment of its glad melody, letting it beat upon his ears as though he could drink a song to satisfy a thirst. He was no longer tired, for the music welled up in him, filling his aching muscles with new life even while he was intent upon its sharp impact with his brain. . . . They came, those notes, in a sequence that was inevitable; foreordained, one followed another into the waiting expectancy of time, and were one missing their sequence would be incomplete, like an unfinished thought, or a sentence with a word left out. . . . Silver notes, jingling in wild rhythms with coppery notes pounding in slow measures down below. Silver notes, dancing against the eardrums, trying to get in, but always just outside. . . . If one could only let them in instead of leaving them to patter painfully against the eardrums—the big notes got in and reverberated between your ribs, but damn it all, the little notes bounced off and hurt . . . dancing notes that fell across the sky like golden sparks slanting over velvet blackness. . . .

"What's the matter?" Joel looked at the Padre, who was shaking him violently by the shoulder.

"How long have you been asleep, man?"

"I wasn't asleep! I was watching the sparks falling——"

"Sparks? Where have you seen any sparks?"

Joel looked up but there was only a grey muggy mist, so he joined sheepishly in the Padre's laughter. He saw that sailors were moving about on the deck behind him, unwinding ropes and letting steam noisily into the windlasses. An officer came up the forecastle-ladder; after a brief glance at the two of them standing in the bow, he muttered an injunction to a sailor and moved to the back edge of the deck where he stood as though waiting for a signal.

The ship drifted slowly past her neighbours, some of which were so close that one could have talked in a quiet voice across the intervening space. Here and there a man leaned out to watch them indifferently, or raised his hand in a friendly gesture. Joel suddenly realized that he was cold and a violent shiver made him turn up his collar and button his coat. He heard a bell sound on the bridge and someone called, "Let go!" The officer echoed, "Let go!" The starboard windlass creaked as a sailor released the brake around the windlass-drum and metal grated on metal beneath their feet where the anchor-chain moved forward a little. Then the chain moved again and began to run out with such a screeching, crashing, roaring noise that the men had to cover their ears. When it was over, Joel recalled that he had not heard the anchor hit the water; he had expected it to make a great splash but it was completely lost in the ear-splitting thunder of that mad chain. He turned to the Padre with a shrug, relieved to be again in silence.

"At last! There was a time when I thought that we would never get here! We've sat up a long time to get that drink. Come on——"

The Padre stopped him with a hand upon his arm.

"Wait a minute. . . . If you put me back among the beasts, what becomes of my life—has it no goal, no purpose?"

Joel looked for a moment at the Padre's hand, which had closed into a tight grip over his arm. He studied the long brown fingers, which held him with an arresting tension as the words echoed in his ears: "Has it no goal, no purpose? Purpose?" . . . The fingers relaxed, and Joel turned away to lean again upon the bulwark. A boat was moving slowly out from the shadow of the bow, pulling an enormous hawser to a buoy. Making her fast! How good it was, after the open sea, to be bound again to something permanent, resting from the unceasing voyaging onward and on-

ward across trackless wastes, through time and space—
how good it was, if it were only to rest and voyage
again. . . . He rubbed his hand over his forehead and
straightened up.

"Must we for ever be like children, seeking purpose
in the fall of the rain, in the sweep of the wind, in the
strike of the lightning! Why must we always seek it in
ourselves? . . . No, your life has no more purpose than
that of any other beast. . . . It has no purpose except
as you choose to give it one. I give you, in the very nature
of life itself, in the momentum that keeps it spinning on its course, an unquenchable instinct for self-
determination—if you wish to call it that; and in the
flesh which life accumulates around itself I give you the
capacity to learn by experience and to test your knowledge by experiment. Is that not enough? . . . But I
cannot give you any personal, predetermined significance. You are only a branch of the stream that is flowing on, resisting the world about it, trying——"

"There it is!" the Padre interrupted. He was smiling,
his eyes fixed upon the faint colours of the morning
sky. "—trying different ways of living, in order to keep
alive! Perhaps in my obscure corner of Africa I can
experiment, too. Perhaps—" he pressed Joel's arm with
a friendly gesture as he moved away, "—well, anyway I
hope I don't turn out to be a blind alley! Come along—

you have sat up long enough to get that drink. You've earned it!"

Joel watched the priest with a puzzled frown as he walked across the deck. His resounding footsteps seemed to echo some familiar phrase, and Joel stopped to listen; but it was not until they had died away that his memory captured it. He chuckled to himself—it was the pulse of life, it had escaped again!